Praise for THE BOOK OF X

"There are very few good reasons to use the word *oneiric* in a sentence and here is one of them: It's one of the few English adjectives appropriate to Sarah Rose Etter's novel about a woman born with a stomach disfigurement who navigates the world (as we all do) with the trepidation and fury and occasional exultation that results from having a disappointing body."
—Molly Young, *Vulture*, The Best Books of 2019

"Both conceptually and stylistically like nothing I've read before… *The Book of X* glimmers like a cracked mirror reflecting our own grotesque features. It is a novel that stays with you long after you've put it down."
—Kali Fajardo-Anstine, *Electric Literature*

"It is a strange, uncanny world, that features the strange and broken body of a strange and broken young woman named Cassie, the narrator we simultaneously pull for, are fascinated by, and want to protect somehow. This is one of the most visceral books I've ever read and one that stays with you long after you've read the last page."
—Robert Lopez, *The Believer*

"At its heart, Etter's is a coming-of-age novel about difference, the female body, and the male gaze, but the author's surreal imagination and laser-precise prose make for an indelible read."
—James Tate Hill, *Lit Hub*

"Sarah Rose Etter's *The Book of X* is dizzying and grotesque—and I say that with the utmost love. It's an astute exploration of humanity and the body—specifically the female body—through the lens of young Cassie… Etter has built an eerie, surreal world… and she seduces you into it with dreamy lyricism. You won't want to leave."
—Arianna Rebolini, *BuzzFeed*

"Etter writes her weird world with elastic
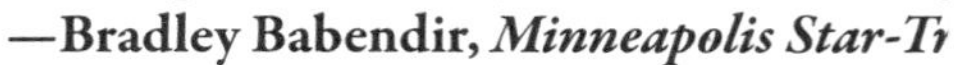
certain points as it is lyrical in others… a
—Bradley Babendir, *Minneapolis Star-Tr*

The Book of X

A NOVEL

Sarah Rose Etter

Two Dollar Radio
Books too loud to Ignore

WHO WE ARE Two Dollar Radio is a family-run outfit dedicated to reaffirming the cultural and artistic spirit of the publishing industry. We aim to do this by presenting bold works of literary merit, each book, individually and collectively, providing a sonic progression that we believe to be too loud to ignore.

TwoDollarRadio.com

Proudly based in
Columbus
OHIO

Love the ***PLANET?*** So do we.

Printed on Rolland Enviro.
This paper contains 100% post-consumer fiber, is manufactured using renewable energy - Biogas and processed chlorine free.

PCF

Printed in the USA

ISBN→ 9781937512811

Library of Congress Control Number available upon request.

Also available as an Ebook.
E-ISBN→ 9781937512828

Book Club & Reader Guide of questions and topics for discussion is available at twodollarradio.com

SOME RECOMMENDED LOCATIONS FOR READING *THE BOOK OF X*:
Near a river, a graveyard, in outer space, or pretty much anywhere because books are portable and the perfect technology!

AUTHOR PHOTO→ by Katie Webb

COVER ARTWORK→ by Paw Grabowski

WE MUST ALSO POINT OUT THAT THIS IS A WORK OF *FICTION*. Names, characters, places, and incidents are products of the author's lively imagination. Any resemblance to real events or persons, living or dead, is entirely coincidental.

Are you living in hell?
Well, try to make the most of it.

—Carol Rama

The Book of X

PART I

I WAS BORN A KNOT LIKE MY MOTHER and her mother before her. Picture three women with their torsos twisted like thick pieces of rope with a single hitch in the center.

The doctors had the same reaction each birth: They lifted our slick warped bodies into the air and stared, horrified.

All three of us wailed, strange new animals, our lineage gnarled, aching, hardened.

Outside, beyond the bright white lights of the hospital, the machine of the world kept grinding on, a metal mouth baring its teeth, a maw waiting to clench down on us.

"I'M NOT RELIGIOUS, BUT I DAMN WELL prayed," my mother says, exhaling smoke over the kitchen table. "I rubbed the rosaries raw that you would take after your father."

My mother's knot rests against the kitchen table. In my tender moments, I want to reach out and place a hand there.

"But as soon as you crowned, I knew it," my mother says. "I could feel your knot."

When my mother tells this story, I take long sips of my lemonade to keep quiet. I know she screamed the whole birth. I brought her the same pain she brought her mother.

"Your father says I went possessed. My eyes rolled back into my head."

THERE ARE 4,500 DIFFERENT TYPES OF knots. There are 3,800 basic variations of these knots. There are an infinite number of ways to combine these knots and their variations. In this way, knots are like stars.

We could have been complicated: Figure eights, clove hitches, sheet bends, reefs, heaving lines.

But our knots are simple: Overhand. Our abdomens twist in and out just once, our bodies wrapping back into themselves, creating dark caverns, coiled as snakes.

IN OLD BLACK-AND-WHITE PHOTOS, MY young mother poses next to my grandmother. Both conceal their knots beneath billowing blouses, standing stiffly on a gray lawn, their gray lips strained into gray smiles over gray teeth.

THE ACRES WERE PASSED DOWN TO MY father from his father and his father before him. A small black sign with white paint says The Acres where our land begins.

We have an old white house and a rust-red barn. Our white house is all wooden floors, arched windows, linens to wash. Our barn is where the sleeping machines are kept.

The rest of the town stands a few miles back from us and our land. We are isolated in this way. Some days, only my family can see me, which is my freedom — no new stares, no new disgust.

The Acres are worth money is what my parents say. Here is why: At the edge of our land is the Meat Quarry. There, meat is harvested from the tall walls of a red, fleshy canyon.

MY MOTHER AND I KEEP THE HOME ON weekends. My mother is like weather in that she changes daily. Each day, I make a report of her.

Today, my mother is focused and sharp, training me to clean. Everything must be white, pristine, diamond. Specks of dirt taunt her.

A bucket of lemons rests at my feet. To keep a home, one must have hands and skin of citrus.

"Now, do it how I do it," she says. "You're old enough for a knife now."

I have seen it: Her back hunched over the sink, the brown of her hair glinting in the sunlight, the fat of her upper arms warbling, the sawing, then the halves between her fingers, yellow half-moons in her palms, rubbing lemon over white wall.

I hunch over the silver gut of the sink. I cut the lemons down the center, one by one, arms shivering against the knife, separating the small citrine hearts.

I run the yellow halves over the white walls until they glisten, until the house tangs with the flesh of the fruit, until the juice of the citrus runs into the gutters of my gnawed nail beds then stings.

EACH DAY, MY FATHER AND BROTHER PULL meat from the quarry to sell in town like my father's father and his father before him. Their bodies disappear over the green grass of The Acres, their figures swallowed by the thin mouth of the long horizon.

I have never seen the Meat Quarry, so I must invent it over and over again in my mind: Giant red walls of flesh marbled with the electric white of fat.

"You're not meant to be there," my father says. "Some things, a woman should not see."

Has my mother seen it? I do not know.

"Does the meat glisten and glitter?"

"Enough. You keep far from there," my father says. "It's not safe."

He drinks his liquor after dinner, eyes going red. My mother's fury hangs at the edge of the table, growing with each sip he takes.

"Haven't you had enough?" she asks.

"What does the quarry smell like?" I ask.

"Enough again," he says sharply. "Both of you, drop it."

MY MOTHER SITS NEXT TO ME ON WICKER porch furniture. We have finished our cleaning for the day. Now, it is magazine time.

My mother's magazines are bright portals to new worlds. Women wear fantastic clothing, their faces dazzling up from the pages.

My mother reads me the new tips.

"This season, women need whiter teeth."

I look at her teeth, their yellowing from years of smoke.

"Another trend is plastic fingernails. Now would you look at these?"

On the page in her lap, a pair of slender hands holds a glass of soda with a straw. The hands have long, bright red nails, shining, luscious, more perfect than anything I have seen before.

I look at her hands, their nails, which are short, unpainted, best for working lemon against wall.

The sun begins its fat drop into the horizon. A thin sadness leaks from my heart for her.

"One day, we'll have white teeth and red nails, too," I say.

Then I invent us like that in my mind: Our teeth gleaming, our nails red. I picture us beautiful, unknotted.

LATER, IN MY BEDROOM, I SHED MY clothes and take inventory of my body in the long mirror.

I am thin at the arms and legs, wiry brown hair down to my shoulders. My eyes are brown, flat. My jaw is large, my ears too big.

My breasts are small, and there is a bit of flatness before it begins. Just below my ribs, the skin changes. My knot is strained and stretch-marked, shining and hard.

I used to gasp when I saw it, but now it is my familiar. I have seen my mother's, too, when she is changing, through the crack in the door. Her breasts sag over her knot. We are different in that way.

The cool air pushes in through the window and runs over that secret skin, a relief in that touch.

AT TIMES, I IMAGINE IT ALL DIFFERENT. Bright visions rush over me, scenes from a golden life in another world.

VISION

Alone, I shed my clothes and take inventory of my body in the long mirror.

I am thin at the arms and legs, brown hair down to my shoulders, bright eyes. I have small breasts, and just below my ribs, my stomach is flat.

I run my hands over my belly, skin smooth as a stone from a river.

The cool air pushes in through the window and runs over my skin, a pleasure in that touch.

I DIG THROUGH MY MOTHER'S OLD MAG-azines in the attic. I flip through the old trends, admire the smooth women.

Tips are written in bold fonts:

YELLOW IS THE COLOR OF THE SEASON

EAT LESS NOW WITH THE ROCK DIET

NEW NAILS, NEW TEETH, NEW LIFE

In the stack, I find an old science magazine. My eyes stutter over the cover.

My mother is younger, holding me in her arms. The title says ***THIRD GIRL BORN KNOTTED***.

Inside, there are pictures of my small body slick with blood and then clean, swaddled in white cloth. My knot is at the center of each photo.

Third Girl Born Knotted; Doctors Halt Research

A third infant has been born knotted to a family in the South. This rare genetic abnormality has flummoxed the medical community.

The first woman, *Eleanor X*, was born a knot in 1947. She gave birth to two sons (unknotted), and a daughter who carried the knot. Her births were not compromised by the knot. In fact, in all three women, the womb is located at the base of the deformity, providing a clear path for birthing.

Her daughter, *Deborah X*, also delivered one daughter and one son. The daughter, *Cassandra X*, was born a knot. The son, again, was born unknotted.

This very rare gene resides on the *X* chromosome. Doctors have determined the knots are largely a cosmetic issue, potentially rendering the women outsiders in society. The impact is largely emotional, rather than physical. Doctors have decided to halt their inquiry into its cause after years of inconclusive research.

I don't hear the footsteps of my mother.

"You should be cleaning. What are you doing?"

"Just looking at your old magazines."

But she catches a glimpse. Today, she is vicious. Her brown eyes flash then froth, rabid. She slaps the journal to the ground. Then her palm stings across my cheek in a quick flash of red.

"Some things are private!"

Her body disappears into the blackness of the doorway. The attic goes silent.

Face red, I look at the ground where a single photo has fallen from between the pages of the journal.

It is a picture of us together.

I am swathed in more fabric than usual. My brother clenches an arm around me. My mother wears a flowered dress, her own knot hidden. My father stands off to the side as if he has been sold a bad car. We are all squinting beneath a bright sun that is just out of frame.

WEEKDAYS, I GO TO SCHOOL. I WALK THE mile. The school is green with a pitched roof.

Most days, no one minds me. I stay quiet to keep it that way.

I keep track of the facts, though.

In my classes, I learn about the human body and history and the human brain, deep seas, jungles, islands, and the distant cities beyond our town and the distant planets beyond our world.

- An octopus has three hearts, nine brains, and blue blood
- Female lions do 90% of the hunting for their pride
- The heart of the blue whale is so large that a human could swim through its arteries
- One square centimeter of skin contains roughly 100 pain sensors
- The sun will only get brighter before it collapses

WHILE I'M IN SCHOOL, MY FATHER AND my brother work the meat from the quarry with their hands and their shovels. That's what my brother says.

On Saturdays, my mother and I clean the meat in the big silver sink. On meat cleaning days, watery pink rivers rush off the flesh. The fresh piles of meat rise like bloody castles on the counter.

On Saturdays, we must act very proper because we must take the meat into town. This is a ritual that requires preparation: I clean myself and put on my best dress. I am like the meat in this way.

In the evening, we drive into town, the clean flesh piled in the truck bed.

"Ten gold coins! Twenty gold coins! Thirty gold coins!" bid the men in the town. Their stomachs and guts are large but knotless. They avert their eyes from us or else they stare too long and too hard at our shapes.

I often imagine a man with a body like mine, a man I might marry.

"Do men ever get knots?" I ask.

"Lower your voice. And no. A man has never had a knot. That is a woman's burden."

"SOLD!" my father bellows.

The men scoop the clean meat into their own buckets, red and raw, the smell of wet coin in the air.

SOMETIMES, MY FATHER BRINGS UP THE old days.

"My father bought this land for a song. Back then, it was harder to tell which lands would have meat."

"Nobody thought this land did?" I ask.

"Sure didn't. Dad knew better though. He could hardly keep the grin off of his face when they were signing the papers. He always told me his gut knew we'd hit it big."

"How did he find the Meat Quarry?"

"Well, everyone in town thought he was a fool," my father says. "In the early days, he crawled the land himself, waiting for the feeling in his gut to grow stronger, belly against the soil."

I move closer to my father. His eyes are not too red yet, the scent of the liquor faint. This is the nicest time to be close.

"It took him two weeks of that. He was on the 13th day when he started to lose faith. But he kept crawling. On the last day, it was raining, and he was out there in the mud, searching."

"How did he know when he'd found it?"

"He said his gut lit up bright, and the hairs on the back of his neck stood up. Said he'd never felt anything like that before."

"Like instinct?"

"Like instinct. Your brother has it too, even stronger than I do. But boy, did it save my father's ass. Everyone in this goddamn town thought he was a joke. Now, we've got the best meat on this side of the river."

LATER, ALONE, I LIE ON MY BELLY IN THE center of my bedroom. My knot presses against the carpet.

I practice my sensing: eyes closed, reaching out with my gut to see where new meat might be on our land.

I wait for the hairs to stand up on the back of my neck. I sense as hard as I can. I feel nothing.

AT SCHOOL, THE OTHER STUDENTS SUR-round me. Their round faces bobble like bad balloons, screaming.

"LOOK AT HER! LOOK AT THE FREAK!"

Their bodies are lanky, pimpled, letting off new odors. Their voices echo off the metal lockers. Their eyes are all on me: blue, brown, green, gray, each eye making my flesh shiver, everyone an enemy.

"YEAH, LOOK AT ME!" I yell back.

I pull up my dress, bare my weak fangs, my knot bright in the sunlight streaming through the windows, a single eye of flesh daring them all to move, to come closer, to try me.

VISION

I'm the queen now. All the students surround me with their offerings at lunch.

"I've brought you an orange," says a boy with one lazy eye.

"Thank you," I say. "That's very kind."

"I've brought you crackers with cheese in the center," says a girl in a plaid dress.

"Wonderful."

They come forward one by one, each with a treat. I smooth my own dress down over my flat stomach. The offerings rise up around me, growing like sweet palaces.

IN BED THAT NIGHT, I SLIDE MY HANDS down. I run my fingers over my knot.

I try to tell myself I don't mind it so much. Under the light of the moon, I picture my teeth growing into big fangs. I widen my mouth, let them catch the breeze. I close my eyes and try to believe, half-girl, half-snake.

THE NEXT MORNING, MY MOTHER SITS at the kitchen table. Her yellow house dress tents over her knot, big as a cheap sun. I spoon cereal into my mouth.

"Will you call the doctor?" I ask. "Will you ask him to unknot me?"

"That's not how it works," my mother says, smoking. "And it's the weekend. They don't work on weekends."

"Why don't you ever try?"

"We've been over this. The doctors don't give a damn about it."

"They screamed at me again. At school."

"I used to spit at them when they spat at me," my mother says.

Then she stares out the window into the long horizon as if in a deep trance, as if staring into another time, as if I were not there, never born.

THAT AFTERNOON, WE'RE IN THE LIVING room. We are cleaning again.

"These curtains are a mess!" my mother says.

She lifts the fabric of the curtains like strange brocade hair.

"And now what is this?"

She pulls one of my father's bottles from the ground, half-full of liquor.

"Motherfucker," she whispers. "Motherfucker."

She slams the bottle on the living room table, then sits down beside me on the couch, so close our knees bang. We face the bottle. Anger shimmers off of her in hot waves. I stay quiet. I know how this goes.

"Now," she says, "we wait for this motherfucker."

The sun sets, and the moon rises. We fall asleep on the couch. When the sun rises again, my father still hasn't come home.

"Time to get ready for school," my mother says.

She slides the bottle back behind the curtain, a strange magic trick, the evaporated day.

VISION

My father has special places for the bottles: Behind the toilet, in the back of the truck, beneath the pillows of the fancy sofa, beneath the chair in the living room, in the shower, in the trash can.

"You're hiding them everywhere," I say. "I found one behind my bed last night."

"It's not what you think. Please don't tell your mother," he says.

"It is too what I think. What will she say when she finds out?"

"You can't tell her. You can't, I'll stop."

The world will spin on as it does until you do something to change it. I pull each bottle from its special place. I stack the glass bottles, half-full of clear liquid, on the front lawn, in the sun.

The pile is bigger than the front door, bigger than the truck. I hurl my body at the pile of glass and begin to smash the bottles one by one, shards glinting in the sun like a new future.

AT NIGHT, I LAY MY HEAD IN MY mother's lap.

"Unknot me," I sob. "Please make someone fix me."

"There's nothing we can do," she murmurs.

"Kill me then," I say. "Please."

My mother exhales smoke, stubs out her cigarette, then puts her cool hand on my forehead, a rare touch.

WHEN THE HOUSE IS SILENT, I SNEAK into my father's office. This is my favorite place.

The room bursts with him. The shelves are lined with his favorite objects: Paused lava rocks, bleached-white bones, books about meat, empty bottles that catch and refract the light like diamonds.

I sit at his desk in his red leather chair. I spin the chair a few times. I open his desk drawer. The silver key to the Meat Quarry gates glistens against the black liner. I clench my fingers around that cool metal until it aches, then slide the key back into the drawer.

A map of the Meat Quarry lines the office wall behind me. The quarry is mapped like veins of a heart: fat arteries, thin arteries, all connected and winding. Areas with the best meat are marked with a red *X*.

I run my fingers over the map, trace the arteries, memorizing paths until I hear the front door open. I sneak out, heart in my throat.

EACH DAY AT SCHOOL, I STARE AT BODIES, memorizing their limbs, their smooth lines. The body of Sophia is my favorite.

A PORTRAIT OF SOPHIA: LONG BROWN hair which shimmers where mine is dull, narrow shoulders where mine are gangly, long legs, no knot where I am knotted.

IN THE MORNINGS, SOPHIA WALKS SLOWLY into the classroom as if covered in sleep. Sophia wears a red dress, then a blue dress, then a green dress. In the afternoons, Sophia laughs in the lunchroom, and light bounces off the white of her teeth. Sophia knows a joy I do not know.

I watch Sophia move and I want to move like she does. Some days, Sophia catches me staring and waves. Sometimes, I lift my limp hand and wave back.

I don't know if my wave tells the truth, which is: *I want to move like you do. I want to slice you open with a knife. I want to hide my body inside of yours.*

TODAY, MY MOTHER WANTS TO HELP. SHE closes my bedroom door behind her then sits beside me on the bed. The heat of her breath scorches my face.

Close up, her wrinkles are deep canyons. I imagine myself walking through the chasms of her skin.

"We need to do something about your looks," she says, running a hand through my hair. "Let's start with the clothes. The magazines say yellow is the color this season."

She walks to my closet and pulls out an old yellow dress made of lace. I shake my head.

"Put it on! It's fun to try new looks."

"I hate this dress. It's too hot."

"Just do it!"

I strip off my old blue dress. I slip the yellow fabric over my head. She yanks up the zipper and the bright lace tents around my knot.

"Now these," she says, wrapping a single strand of pearls around my neck. The pearls are tight, hot, plastic.

She walks me into her bedroom. We are surrounded by her special creams, the ghost of her perfume, facing her big mirror.

"There now," she says. "Isn't this just perfect? Shouldn't we do this every day? Let's take a picture!"

IN THE PHOTOGRAPH, I STAND NEXT TO her mirror in the dress and the pearls. My eyes are red as if I have been crying, as if I want to remove the pearls, the dress, my skin.

OUT UNDER THE BURNING SUN, MY brother digs the red meat up out of the earth, filling silver bucket after silver bucket after silver bucket. I imagine it that way. Then he is showered, clean, in fresh clothes at the dinner table.

"Big day in the quarry today," he says.

We fork bland cubes of meat into our mouths.

"It takes a gut instinct, son," my father says. "And you have it. Boy, I wish I had it like you."

The room falls silent after this rare praise. My mother exhales a plume of smoke. The meat takes on the scent.

AFTER DINNER, I CUT THE FLAT-stomached women out of my mother's magazines.

They wear bathing suits or dresses cut in at the hip. Slicing the pages gives me peace, silver metal humming through the paper until the women are separated from their scenes.

Inside the dim light of my bedroom closet, I tape their torsos to the wall, floor to ceiling. I call them The Sophias. They are the girls a boy would like to touch.

ONE DAY, SOPHIA SPEAKS. SHE IS WEARING a pink dress, the light from her mouth making her hair and her eyes and her skin brighter.

"Why do you always stare?" she asks. "I hate it."

"I wish I looked like you," I blurt.

"No, you don't," she says. "It's all the same no matter how you look."

The lie makes her a friend.

I BEGIN TO BRING SOPHIA TO THE ACRES each day after school. We spend afternoons exchanging secrets, whispering about boys. We nod into each other's hair.

"Let me see your knot," she says one day.

I don't fight. I stand in the center of the living room and lift my dress up slow as an ache. In the afternoon sun, my knot looks even worse, each stretchmark illuminated.

"Well," she says flatly. "That's disgusting. Pull your dress down."

I sit back on the couch, dying inside, until she puts an arm around me, and whispers in my ear.

"I think I saw Jarred staring at you today."

JARRED IS TALLER THAN THE OTHERS AT school, lanky bodied. His hair is short, uneven, cut over a kitchen sink. A dirty streak of freckles crosses his nose, cheeks.

Under his skin is an anger that casts a shadow around him.

"Why are you always looking at me?" he asks.

I lift my eyes and stare right into his face.

That's when I realize it: His left eye is lazy, the pupil unfocused, staring off into another world. His right eye pierces into me like a knife.

I TELL SOPHIA WHAT'S IN MY INSIDES.

"It's awful inside of me," I say.

"What's in there?" she asks.

"I have a pit of badness in my stomach," I say.

Then we sit in the quiet of the confession.

VISION

Under the fluorescent lights, I am gaping wide. My incision is wide and long, from hip to hip, across my flat belly, right where a woman would grow a baby.

With each breath, black blood gurgles out from the slit. My insides are no longer red. Now, my organs are black, no longer soft, now covered in dark sparkling crystals.

I can't stop looking at my terrible insides, at how wretched I have become there, how beautiful the rot is.

My wound keeps glittering with each breath, a terrible evening of stars shimmering inside of me.

EACH WEEK, MY MOTHER TAKES ME TO visit the bodies of my grandparents. We walk to the edge of The Acres where there is a cemetery squared by a low white fence.

"It keeps the wolves out," my mother says.

Crooked white crosses spell out their names in script above the dates of birth and death. We place small offerings on low grassy mounds.

"They'll love this," my mother whispers.

The offerings: Flowers, small sugar cookies, rosaries, a small cheap statue of an angel. Against the crosses, the gifts look wrong. They will spoil in the rain, melt down to strange, warped blobs of colored sugar and plastic.

"Now, isn't this nice?"

My mother sits between the graves and caresses the grass.

"I just miss you so much," she says to the ground, her sob a fist which clenches the heart in my chest.

I leave her side, wander the edge of the cemetery. My eyes land on a black shape beneath the grass, a rocky mound. I lean down. It is a tiny tombstone, smaller than the crosses.

Stephen X
B: Jan 3
D: Jan 5

"Don't look at that," my mother hisses. "Get over here, that doesn't concern you."

"Who is it? Who is Stephen?"

"Who do you think it is? Use your head."

A hollow feeling enters my chest and stays there through the drive home, through dinner, until I am in my bed, wrapped in my sheets, still as a body in a grave.

VISION

My father guides the truck over the land through the town to the big cemetery. Here, the strangers are buried. The sun is fat and hot in the blue sky.

"You ready to play our favorite game?" my father asks.

"Yes! Let's play it!"

He stops the truck and we climb out. The steel black gate lets out a low moan when he unlatches it. We step into the cemetery, long green grass sprouting up between the headstones which jab up out of the ground like strange granite teeth.

"And... GO!" my father shouts.

I work my way through the cemetery, weaving through the graves. I get lost in the names, the small tombstones.

My father is always faster than I am. He starts shouting his numbers. "1913! 1908! 1898!"

I shout mine back once I catch up, heart pounding. "1916! 1884! 1911!"

"1879!" my father yells, and he is the winner.

We climb back into the car. He puts a very sad song on the stereo and hums along as he drives us to the ice cream store, the second part of our ritual.

"I'll still buy you one," my father says.

We both buy vanilla. We don't speak on the drive home, just listen to the very sad song again and again as he navigates us home.

ONE AFTERNOON IS DIFFERENT FROM the rest. Sophia and I are alone in the house, which is quiet. I like the silence like that, a blanket.

"I want to teach you a new game," Sophia says. "I learned it from Jarred. Let's go into your bedroom."

In the dull afternoon light, she climbs into my bed with me.

She slides her knee between my legs.

"This is called rocking horse," she says. "Jarred loves this game."

Then she moves her leg until my face flushes and my body trembles, until pink sweetness explodes from between my legs and floods my veins.

AT LUNCH, I CHEW A SANDWICH. JARRED does the same. His eyes catch mine. We lock gazes until he slams his sandwich down on the table.

My pulse quickens as he walks to my table. He gets close enough to drop his head to mine, his lips near my ear.

"Stop looking at me, you fucking freak," he whispers. "You're disgusting."

He walks back to his seat and sits down. I keep my head down, fill my mouth again with bread.

VISION

I go straight for my father's tools. I find a screwdriver and a pair of pliers. The tools are heavy and cold in my hand. I trust metal.

In my bedroom, I strip off my clothes. The pliers in my right hand, the screwdriver in my left. I wrap the mouth of the pliers around the first twist of the knot. I jam the screwdriver into the knot's crevice.

I pull with all of my might, my teeth grinding against each other. I want the pliers and the screwdriver to splinter me, I want to undo myself. Blood rushes from my knot in thick red streams.

My bedroom door opens, and my mother fills the doorway.

"What are—" she starts. Then she is on me, ripping the tools from my hands.

"What is wrong with you?" she demands.

"I want it gone!" I scream. "I want to be like Sophia!"

My mother puts me into the bath, both of us silent, only the pink water making sound. Soon I'm surrounded by the warm water, eyes closed. Then my mother's hand is on my cheek.

SOPHIA LIVES CLOSER TO THE SCHOOL. She takes me home one afternoon. At her house, everything is proper.

Her mother is in the den. Her mother is a thin, sharp woman. She is precise as a knife. She says, "No sugar, remember," and hands us carrots to eat.

At Sophia's house, there are rules about sugar, screaming, laughing too loud. We go to Sophia's room, which is pristine and pastel pink. We sit on her bedroom floor. I confess again.

"I feel so sad some days," I whisper.

Pain has been welling up inside of me: My knot makes me other.

"What do you mean?" she asks.

I run a hand over my stomach. I feel as if I am from another planet.

"I just want someone to take it away," I say.

Sophia nods. In her eyes, I see a big warmth which expands. She reaches out and touches my hand. My pain becomes a bit smaller. We don't play rocking horse at Sophia's house, but there is this.

I WALK WITH MY BROTHER INTO THE Acres. The land stretches all around us. My brother carries his mallet and shovel. He's meant to test my instinct.

"How do you know where the meat will be?" I ask my brother. "Teach me how to sense."

"Dunno," he says. "It's like I have a magnet in my gut and it pulls me there."

"Find one then," I say.

We keep walking until a small hum comes from my brother's mouth. It sounds like the thrum of metal.

"Here," he murmurs.

The ground is nothing but sparse dirt. I stomp a foot to be sure. It feels no different than any other land under foot.

"No, no. Don't do that."

His breath quickens. He stands strong on a certain spot. His fingers move to the buttons on his shirt and he undoes them one by one. Bare chested, he lifts his mallet into the air above his head and brings it down to the ground.

The earth shakes with the puncture. The mallet leaves a deep dent in the dirt.

"Let's take a look," he says.

We bend over the new hole, stare down into the deep dirt.

"See, the dirt gets redder at the bottom. Step back."

He lifts the mallet again and drops it once more into the same hole, driving deeper this time.

We lean over the hole again, which slowly fills with red liquid. Blood rises up from the meat below to the upper crust of the soil.

"Red never lies," he says, grinning. "That's how you know."

He grabs his shovel and digs. Blood rushes forth with each new slice into the earth. Soon, he is covered in it. My brother keeps digging and digging, down to the meat, a slick machine.

TODAY, MY MOTHER IS FOCUSED ON illusion.

"We must do something about your face," she says.

I follow her voice into the yellow light of her bathroom.

"Look at you," she says. "You're a mess."

She pulls her makeup from the cabinet. Small pots of color cover the counter alongside sharp silver instruments, black brushes.

"Let's start with the eyebrows," she says.

She brings a thin pair of tweezers to my face. She grasps a single hair and pulls. Tears well up in my eyes.

"It hurts!"

"Too bad," she says. "We can't have you walking around like this. People talk, you know."

She keeps going, keeps pulling the hairs from my brows, one by one. Each yank is a small torture. Water streams down my face, which becomes red and blotchy in the mirror.

"Now let's do the rest," she says.

Her fingers run over my face, then a brush, then another brush, I am a painting.

"There now," she says. "Open your eyes."

I don't recognize myself. I am another girl from another planet, a warped version of myself.

SOPHIA STARTS TO DO BAD THINGS.

First, she steals lip gloss from the store in town.

"You just put it in your bra," she says, then she puts it in her bra.

When I try, the lip gloss slides over my braless chest and catches on my knot before it falls to the ground.

SOPHIA IS ALSO SMOKING.

She smokes the butt of a found cigarette on the walk home from school each day, coughing.

"You just purse your lips and inhale," she says, smoking.

I take a drag and cough like her.

"Nice," I say, smoking.

SOPHIA HAS ALSO BEEN KISSING THE BOYS. Everyone knows about it.

"Sophia's a slut," the girls whisper to me in the hall. "Sophia's a total hoe."

She kisses the boys with the plain brown hair by the dumpsters after lunch.

"It's no big deal," Sophia says, smoking. "It's just mouths."

I think about the smell of rotting lunches in the dumpsters. Then I think about Jarred's mouth on mine.

- Two-thirds of people tilt their head toward the right when they kiss
- The muscle used to pucker the lips is called *orbicularis oris*
- The word *kiss* is derived in part from the Old English *cyssan*, "to touch with the lips" in respect or reverence
- No two lip prints are the same
- In medieval times, it was common to sign the name with an *X*, then kiss the mark as a display of sincerity

I BEGIN TO TRICK JARRED INTO TOUCH-ing me. I stand in the middle of the hallway each morning when his bus arrives.

He enters the building in the stream of other bodies, bookbag slung over his shoulder. Morning still crusts his eyes.

I hold my breath until he gets close, closer, closest, then brushes against my arm and I am lit by a million watts.

"Why are you always in my way?" he hisses.

But I still radiate from it, the contact of our skins. The light of it makes me want.

MY BODY IS A LAND UNDISCOVERED, MY heart beneath the skin wanting to be found and touched.

Between my legs, nothing has happened since rocking horse. Some nights, I slide a pillow there and rock again, thinking of Jarred.

TODAY, MY MOTHER IS FOCUSED ON SELF-improvement.

"Take off your clothes," she says.

We stand in her bedroom.

"I don't want to."

"It's time to look at ourselves with honesty," she says.

My mother has been going into town. She's been spending more money. Her fingernails are made of plastic now. Her teeth gleam whiter than snow.

"Your teeth are so white," I say.

"It's a new technique from the dentist in town," she says. "He is a hunk."

She yanks my dress over my head, then runs her hands over my body, fake plastic nails brushing my shoulders, my arms, my hips, then thighs.

"We need to slim you down," she says.

VISION

I am the queen of the cake room.

There are dozens of round cakes on silver steel tables. Pastel frosting flowers dot their edges and tops. I am starving, My hand sweats around a fork.

I step toward them, mouth full of drool.

The first cake is round, white with pink flowers. I sink the fork into it and pull out a big hunk. In my mouth, the sugar dissolves against my tongue. I'm fast to fork another piece between my lips, the sugar smearing across my cheeks.

I eat and I eat and I eat, the cake filling my stomach. There are cakes everywhere and no one can stop me, not my mother, not my father. I eat, and I eat, and I eat, the sugar rushes through my veins. There are cakes everywhere, and when I'm done with this cake, I can eat another and another and another and no one can stop me.

MY MOTHER HANDS ME A BROWN PAPER bag with a single rock inside.

"This is the latest diet," she says. "Suck on this at lunch. The dirt and meat particles have calories that burn fat in them. I read about it in a magazine."

IN THE CROWDED LUNCHROOM, PLASTIC chairs scrape the floor. The mouths of my classmates open and sandwiches slide in. Jarred eats a peach, the long strings hang from his lips, the deep color of the pit in the blood of the fruit.

I hunger for a peach, a cake, a meat.

I feed myself the future instead: Slender, cheekbones sharp, mouth pursed, thin thighs, thin arms.

I slide the rock into my mouth.

"I WON'T GO OUT INTO THE QUARRY today," my father says at the breakfast table.

His face is strange and gray. A sour smell fevers off of his body.

"What's wrong?" my mother asks, exhaling smoke. "Too much again last night?"

A silence comes down on the table. We wait for a fight like this most days. Some days a fight comes, some days it doesn't. Today, it passes by.

"You're on your own today," he says to my brother. "Go to the side lands and look for a new harvest."

My brother nods. My mother exhales smoke, eyes sharp on my father, dissecting.

"I'm going to see Sophia today," I say.

"Fine," she says. "Get out of our hair."

AFTER BREAKFAST, I SLIP INTO MY father's office. I slide the gate key from his desk drawer. The metal is hot in my hand, my secret lights a fire in my veins, it thrums in my body, my knot humming.

"Goodbye," I shout on my way out the door.

I cross the fields, heart racing. All of the sky big and blue as ever, and I am free in the world. The meat is on the air already, the red wounds of the quarry in the distance. Rings of sweat begin beneath my arms.

A latticed black gate rises up before me, the entrance to the quarry. Through the slits in the gate, I can see glimpses of the meat. I slip the key from my pocket and into the mouth of the lock.

The gate swings open with a long, low creak. The path is shallow at the start, with low red rocky walls on either side.

A small set of tracks lines the ground. Metal carts sit silent and empty. I follow the tracks deeper into the quarry. The earth around me gets redder with each step, the scent of meat filling my nose and mouth.

The red rocks gradually morph, the stench growing stronger, almost choking. Slick wet spirals of meat surround me, rising above my head in high walls, thin veins of white fat running through the redness.

The meat glistens like a rare gem, a beautiful hypnosis. Chunks have been removed from the walls here, places where my brother and father tore the meat from the earth to eat and sell.

I run my fingers over the slickness, get red up to the wrists, lick the blood from my fingers.

I move closer, press my body against the meat, press my mouth against the wall, let the blood soak into my face.

THEY'VE TAKEN ALL THE BOYS AWAY. IT IS time for sexual education.

I sit next to Sophia. We dart eyes at each other until the teacher walks in.

A diagram is on the wall, and it shows the female body, the muscles drawn in beautiful gray lines.

"Today," the teacher says, "we're going to learn about sex."

Nervous laughter pecks up out of our throats. Sophia makes a gagging face at me.

"Now, this is what the inside of your body looks like," the teacher says. "These organs here? They are how you become pregnant after intercourse."

Another burst of laughter comes forward.

"Calm down, now calm down," the teacher says. "We have to get through a lot today. Be mature here."

The teacher glances over at me.

"Oh, oh, I should say," the teacher says. "You're something else altogether. I'm not sure how your body works. Maybe just ignore this."

My throat closes up. I stare down at my desk. Sophia reaches over and pinches me. I look up.

"Fucking shithead," she mouths at me.

"Now, when you have sex with a man, his sperm will travel up the vagina to the uterus then to the cervix," the teacher continues. "If the ovary has created an egg and it is nearby, the sperm can swim to it and enter it. This is called fertilization, and we do *not* want it to happen. I simply cannot stress this enough."

- The uterus is roughly the shape and size of a small pear
- In Ancient Greece, the uterus was believed to be an organ which wandered around the body, causing all emotional and physical female problems
- *Uterus didelphys* is a rare condition which causes women to be born with two uteruses
- One in 4,500 women are born without a uterus
- The uterus is the only organ that can create an entire other organ; during pregnancy, the placenta is grown inside the uterus

WE ARE ALL PILED INTO THE TRUCK. MY mother sits up front next to my father, smoking. My brother stares out the window from the seat beside me as we cross the land.

"River day," she hums. "Are you excited for river day?"

Dread takes root in my gut and grows.

"I don't feel good," I say. "I think I'm getting sick."

The tar of my anxiety spreads through my veins.

"Can we just have a nice day?" my mother snaps.

"I'm sorry," I say.

The river is crowded with the faces of people from town. I see Jarred across the water.

We strip to our swimsuits. Then my mother and I stand next to the river. I can feel the eyes of everyone around us on our knots, on my knot. I flush with shame.

"We came here to swim," my mother says, voice like metal.

My mother pulls my hands from my stomach. We move to the water.

"Isn't this nice?" my mother says, but there's no joy to it.

I dive beneath the water. I go deep, then even deeper. I try to go deep enough to drown the knot.

VISION

The sign at the entrance says: THIGH RIVER PARK. NO TRESPASSING, but Sophia tugs my hand and pulls me in.

We walk down a long path until we reach giant dark rocks.

"We're going to have to climb a little," she says.

She starts to make her way up the rock. I watch her maneuver, then follow her motions. I can hear water in the distance.

"There it is," Sophia says when we reach the top of the rock.

I stare out over the landscape: Rocks and trees surround a river. But the river is the color of many skins. My mind tries to force the hues into logic but cannot.

"The river is full of them today," Sophia says.

As soon as she says it, all of my cells light up with horror-shock, a split second before I start gagging.

The river is full of thighs, pushing along like fish, huge as bass, moving downstream. The thighs bump up against each other, create awkward waves, a strange flood of lone limbs in water, a tide of skin tones rushing by.

"What the fuck?" I ask.

"They're here," Sophia says, pointing.

Boys stand on the rocks across the water, dozens of boys. They wear boxers, their bare chests reflecting the color of the river. Everything is flesh against rock.

I can make out some of their faces. I recognize some of them from school. I make out Jarred's face in the crowd.

Sophia strips off her shorts and t-shirt, unhooks her bra then removes more, her nude body puckering in the cold air.

"Cassie," Sophia whispers through teeth. "Take your clothes off."

I have never been naked in front of boys before.

"Do not fuck this up, prude," Sophia hisses.

The boys howl my name. Jarred says nothing, just stares at me dumbly.

I jerk my legs out of my shorts and stretch my elbows through my t-shirt as I slide it off. I'm normal like Sophia, I have a smooth, flat belly, no knot.

In the river air, my naked body shakes. I go blue like her. When she climbs down the rocks and into the water, I do that too.

The water wraps itself around me, cold, sends shiver shocks through me.

I watch Sophia splay out on her back and float with the thighs.

Her breasts surface up above the water.

I lie back on the water like her. I tilt my head up.

The tide of thighs slides against me, moving past. The thighs touch me, caress me heavily, dozens of them. The feeling of the wet skin is new. The slick slithering makes me dizzy.

I close my eyes and forget the sky. I forget the boys.

A thigh glides past my neck, over my arm, away. Another thigh passes over my calves and down to my toes. Thighs skim my stomach and hips, constantly.

More thighs push their way to new places on my back, brushing parts of my skin that I can never reach, sending electricity from my chest down to the place between my legs.

The mouths on the rock make louder sounds, noises bigger than the river tones, shake me out of myself.

I open my eyes. The boys are clustered on the rocks closest to me, now stripped too.

Their hands are moving against themselves.

The river does not stop. The thighs keep brushing all over me. We keep floating. I keep floating. On the rocks, all of the hands keep moving, all of the eyes on me.

THE MOON IS BIGGER THAN ANY NIGHT before. A wildness in the light keeps me awake.

There's a knock on my window, then it slides open. Sophia's face slides into view.

"Cassieeeeee," she calls softly. "You awake?"

"Yes."

She dangles a silver key in my direction.

"Get up. Come on, come on. Let's go for a ride."

I sneak down the stairs and out of the house, into the night air. Then I follow her to my father's red tractor which looms metallic on the lawn.

Sophia climbs up onto the tractor and gestures for me to follow. Her breath is sour on the night air. She slides a bottle from inside of her jacket and passes it to me.

"You have some catching up to do," she says.

I want to be wild, forget the knot, forget the earth. I chug, and it goes like knives down my throat, then numbs me good.

"Atta girl," she says.

She turns my father's tractor on, the quick roar of the engine, then steers us across the land. The wind runs through our hair.

She hands me the bottle again, and I swig longer and deeper. The numbness builds in my veins, as if the knot has been erased from me. I laugh up at the sky.

"Let's ring the barn!" she yells.

She accelerates, and the seat bounces beneath us, I put my hands in the air, let out a yell.

We circle the red barn at a high speed, Sophia making the tractor turn tighter and tighter. We lean with the machine, we kick up dust around the wheels when we hit the curve.

"WOOOO HOOOOO," she shouts.

The scenery is moving rapidly around me now: The moon, the red wood of the barn, the crisp night sky, the dirt on the ground.

"Slow dow—" I start.

"FUCK," she yells as the tractor takes the next turn too tight, the wheels spinning out beneath us.

We smash through the side of the red barn. The tractor wheels spin out on some hay, then come to a stop. I lift my head, pulse pounding, shaken.

The hole in the barn wall is like a giant mouth. Through its jagged teeth, I can see the moon, the stars, the whole world.

THE SUN HITS OUR FACES THROUGH THE smashed barn wall. My mouth is a mound of sand, tongue dry, stuck to the backs of my furred teeth.

Sophia is beside me, snoring.

I let my elbow find her gut and sink it in.

"Get up, get up, get up," I say.

The air gets a few degrees colder. A shadow falls over us: My mother.

"WHAT THE ACTUAL FUCK NOW?" she screams. "What have you done!? LOOK AT WHAT YOU HAVE DONE!"

Sophia starts laughing.

"And you, what are you doing here?" she asks.

"Just having fun for once," she says.

"FUN?" my mother screams, pulling the bottle from the hay. "You're going home right fucking now, Sophia. And you?"

She turns to me.

"Get to your fucking room."

I bound across the field and up the stairs, into my room, where I lock the door. I climb into my bed, head pounding, dizzy.

- Late Stone Age jugs suggest that intentionally fermented drinks existed during the Neolithic period
- Alcohol is a depressant which in low doses causes euphoria
- In higher doses, alcohol causes stupor, unconsciousness, or death

I SPEND DAYS WITH THE LEMONS, RUB-
bing the walls. I am not allowed on the phone. The hours ache by.

A WEEK LATER, MY MOTHER IS STRANGELY
happy. The fight has worn off of her. We are going shopping.

"Are you ready?" my mother calls, singsong.

I am rotten today, nastiness in my body. My knot feels thicker, more prominent. My mother does not notice. We drive to town.

"What a beautiful day!" she hums.

Mania is a trap. Trees whip past. I count the dead deer on the side of the road.

"What are you thinking about?" she asks.

The bloody ribs of the deer reach up out of their bodies to the sun.

"The ribs of the deer look like fingers," I say.

"Could we try for just a minute not to be disgusting? We're trying to have a nice day and get you a dress."

"Yes," I murmur. "Nice day."

The store is rich and glowing. The lights are thin ribs electric above us. We walk over pristine linoleum floors, the racks of clothing around us pushing in.

"This would be nice!" she says. "How about this one? Oh, let's try this."

She fills her hands with lilac satin, yellow taffeta, a sickening green velvet.

"Won't these be nice?" she asks.

"I don't like those. I like black and red."

"Well, we need to try new things, so we're going to try new things," she says.

In the changing room, the dresses hang behind me like limp bodies.

"Hurry up," my mother calls.

I put on the yellow dress, too tight against my body, a cage. I look sallow, a tumor.

"I don't want to show you this one," I call.

"Stop fucking around," she hisses. "Get out here right now."

I stop fucking around and walk into the dull blare of the lights. A set of three giant mirrors triples my wrong shape, the horrid color, over and over again, infinitely. My mother lets out a sigh.

"This is all wrong. Take it off."

I put on the next dress: An aching lilac satin that strains against me. I step out of the dressing room, teeth bared.

"Is this it?" I bellow. "COULD THIS BE THE ONE?"

"Don't be goddamn ridiculous," my mother hisses. "It looks terrible. Get it off!"

I picture her mouth with duct tape over it, the sky widening with calmness above my head in the bright new silence.

VISION

I stand on our front porch, barefoot, the white house muted behind me. My mother is cleaning inside again, but the scent hasn't reached me yet.

The sky is stormy green, the shade of terror or mold. The wind riles itself up around me, pushing at my skin and hair.

In the secret part of my heart, I think about Jarred, looking at that sky. I only want to whisper into his ear, to feel the curl of his fine hair near my lips.

The wind rolls harder. Inside, the radio chatters warnings. Pressure builds, waiting to drench down thick on the land.

Suddenly, a red dress appears in the sky, a bright slash against the dark gray clouds. I watch as it falls, getting larger as it draws closer to the earth, then drifts onto the grass, empty and thin, collapsing into a pool of fabric.

The sky fills with other dresses in different colors: Blue satin gowns drip down alongside black strapless numbers. Old green chiffon twirls around black and white polka dot dresses until they go weak on the grass.

The sky is a mess of hues and textures, clouds building with the promise of more cloth to come. Tulles and silks and polyesters fall past my face, skirts and bodices billowing.

Each gown lands with a soft thussssh when its fabric collapses against the ground.

I walk through the gown rain until I get to the red dress. I kneel down to the scarlet fabric, running my fingers over it.

The dresses begin to fall faster, the closets of a million women pouring down over me.

Still-glittering prom gowns and wrinkled dark grey sheaths brush against my arms. A heat builds in my belly and below it.

The hues and textures keep falling, combining, coming, puddling. I hear the screen door open.

"You better get your ass inside," my mother screams from the porch.

"I'll be in soon," I call. "Just a minute."

A beige dress brushes past my face. The touch is so light my chest swells with the want to weep.

Jarred, I whisper.

I cannot stop myself. I collapse on the red dress, stretch my body over the slippery fabric, the new touch. I look up at the sky.

The dresses stack up around me, pile down, make weight on top of me. Scents rise up from the threads to greet me, smells of flea markets and old perfume and hidden sweat.

A yellow fabric falls over my nose and mouth like a hand over the face, taking my air. I go dizzy from the lack of oxygen, my eyes close against the fabric, the weight of it like Jarred's body pressing against me.

LOW SOUNDS OF GRUNTING AND panting through my open window wake me in the night.

I follow the sound across the field to the deep red door of the barn.

I crack the door, and I press my eye against the peeling red wood.

Inside, my father is shirtless, covered in blood, bottle by his side. Piles of meat surround him. He shoves a handful of the red into his mouth. His eyes glint with some level of madness.

A small gasp escapes my mouth, and my father's eyes flash up. He's at the door in an instant.

"Well, look what we have here," he slurs. Small flecks of meat land on my cheeks when he speaks. "Spying for your mother, huh?"

"No, I just heard…"

He yanks me into the barn, shutting the door behind us.

"You're going to help me," he says.

"What's going to go—"

"Drink up," he says, handing me the bottle.

I take a swig. It burns clear down the throat.

"This is all gonna go bad soon," he says again.

He sinks his hand deep into the meat and pulls out a clump.

"Get started," he says, handing me the meat.

My throat tightens, but I force my lips open and slide it into my mouth.

I picture snakes in the wild, consuming men whole. I picture women swallowing swords, great sharks consuming millions of fish at once. The meat slides down my tight throat, begins to work through my knot.

"Good," he says. "We won't waste this harvest. We've worked too damn hard."

We eat all night, the bottle between us, an endless midnight dinner, eating until it feels we might split open.

In the morning, in the bathroom mirror, red is smeared across my face. I grin into my reflection, a wild animal.

AT SCHOOL, A PHRASE IS NEWLY scratched into the wood of my desk: KNOTTY BITCH.

Red rushes to my cheeks.

A line-up of my classmates' faces flicks through my head: Jarred, Sophia, the other kid with the lazy eye.

"I know you did it," I hiss at Sophia, pointing at the words on my desk.

"What do you mean?" she asks. "I didn't do anything."

"Just admit it. Just admit you carved it into my desk."

"You're fucked up," she says. "Fuck you."

- The word *knot* comes from the Old English *cnotta*, meaning an intertwining of ropes
- The knot was a symbol of the bond of marriage from the early 13th century
- In the Inca culture, the only "written" language was a system of knots tied into documents called *quipus*, or "talking knots," which recorded numbers, and retold stories and historical events
- Gorillas and select species of birds are known to tie knots

ONE SATURDAY MORNING, MY FATHER pulls me from bed before sunrise.

"Today is the day," he says.

We take the tractor across the land, driving until we reach the entrance to the quarry. My father unlocks the black gate with his key.

"Isn't it incredible?" my father asks, as we step inside, the quarry walls rising up around our heads.

I act awed.

"Yes," I say. "It's bigger than I ever imagined."

My father grips my hand, and we walk deeper into the quarry, following the silver tracks until we come to a split in the path. He gestures to the left.

"Now, this here," he says, "your brother discovered this."

We veer left and the meat scent gets stronger than I remember it before, the red deeper, the rivers of fat thicker, whiter, brighter.

"This is quality," he explains. "You see here how the fat spirals evenly through the flesh? That's going to sell for more every damn time."

We walk until we come to a dead end of meat, a place where the digging has stopped.

"We've got more to do here," he says, gesturing to the last wall. "There's enough here to keep us in money for years. Just have to harvest it. Then watch your mother spend it all."

FOR WEEKS, SOPHIA AND I DO NOT SPEAK.

Our eyes never meet.

ALONE, MY DAYS GET STRANGER.

My vision goes wild. The grass begins to breathe. Through the window at breakfast, the green blades heave, pulsing like a large body below the house.

"The land is alive," I say.

"You're acting weird again," my father says, through the toast in his mouth.

I slide my morning rock into my mouth and suck.

- The loneliest creature on earth is a whale who has been calling for a mate for two decades
- There are roughly 60,000 miles of blood vessels in the human body
- Like fingerprints, each person has a unique tongue print
- It is impossible to commit suicide by holding your breath

I WAKE IN THE MIDDLE OF THE NIGHT, sweat pooling in the curves of my knot.

The empty walls of my stomach grind against each other. I make my way down to the kitchen.

I open the pantry cabinet. Inside, there is a perfect loaf of bread. The hunger makes me wild. I stuff the bread into my mouth, I gorge until it feels like choking.

"GET UP," MY MOTHER SAYS. "WE'RE going to the doctor."

Outside, the sun blares light down on us. A headache begins behind my eyes.

"This doctor is supposed to be very handsome," she says.

"Do you think he can fix me?"

"We'll see," my mother says. "Maybe he fixes us both."

IN HIS OFFICE, I SIT ON THE PADDED table in a paper gown white as frosting, shivering.

The door opens.

"Well, hello there. You must be Cassie," the handsome doctor says. He has brown hair, brown flashing eyes, thick lips, a jaw like the men in the magazines.

I nod.

"Mind if I take a look?"

He slides the gown above the knot. He stares deeply into the caverns, a wonder in his eyes.

"May I touch it?" he asks.

I nod.

The doctor runs his cold fingers over my body.

"Just going to do a few more things here," he says.

He pulls out a measuring tape and measures my knot. He pulls out a flashlight and shines it into the darkest parts of my knot. He uses a small rubber mallet to tap certain sections, testing for reflex.

"Well, we unfortunately have not made enough strides in research to handle this," he says. "There are, however, a few things we can do for now that will make life easier."

"You mean you can't just fix me?"

"We just aren't there yet."

"What can you do for us now?" my mother asks.

"Well, there are some injections that will help loosen the knot and make it easier to operate on later," he says.

"Can you give us a moment?" my mother asks. He nods and leaves the room. Alone with my mother, the walls feel brighter, closer.

"Well, he really is a hunk," my mother says.

"I just—"

"Listen, sweetie, this is all we've got for now," my mother says. "Get the injections."

I picture it: The needles entering me, the knot loosening into a future flat body.

THE DOCTOR KNOCKS AND ENTERS AGAIN, a black case in his hand.

"I had a feeling you'd want to try this," he says.

He shoots a wink at me as he unzips the black leather which opens like a mouth, giant needles for teeth.

"Excellent," he says. "Now just lie down for me."

The first needle appears quickly. He flicks the end with his finger.

"OK, this will hurt a bit. Look up at the ceiling."

He slides up my gown and sinks the needle deep into my knot. A sob begins in my gut, but I imagine my throat full of cotton and hold it there.

He draws another needle and I squirm on the table.

"Now, now," he says.

He sinks the next needle into the knot. He rubs my arm between the shots.

"How many more?"

"We're getting there," he says.

The next needle he sinks into my skin pinches even deeper inside.

"Just 37 more to go," he says.

The doctor begins his own ritual.

"Here comes the sugar water, here comes the sugar water, here comes the sugar water," he murmurs under his breath.

Needle after needle sinks into my body until I lose count.

I WAKE THE NEXT MORNING PINPRICKED. The knot is still there.

My body aches from the injections, from the memory of the needles sinking into my body.

- In 1844, the first hollow needle was invented for injections
- The first hypodermic medical needle was used to introduce morphine into the skin of patients who suffered from sleep disorders
- The word *hypodermic* comes from two Greek words meaning "below skin"

I SIT AT MY SCHOOL DESK IN MY RED dress. I am early. Outside, it is raining. The musk of the rain is in the air, on my clothes, in my mouth.

The classroom door opens and Jarred appears. He sits down next to me.

"Morning," he says.

"Hey."

Then everything shifts.

He stares at me as he lowers his hand to the zipper of his blue pants. The sound of the metal smoothing open rushes through my ears as he pulls out his private self, which is pink as the bellies of the pigs.

He keeps his eyes on me and begins to stroke.

"Look at me," he says.

I feel loose between the legs, dizzy in the head. The classroom with its posters and desks warps around me.

"I said look at me," he commands quietly.

I pull my gaze up to meet his.

We sit like that for some endless time. The scent of his body overtakes the scent of moss. He moves his hand faster and faster until there is a low mean moan and a shudder that shakes the desk in time. His face warps.

I PICTURE US IN THE FUTURE, MARRIED in the small chapel on the edge of town, me with no knot, his face warped with pleasure again.

IT IS SATURDAY, TWO DAYS WITHOUT seeing Jarred, each moment a desert.

I roll out of bed to go to the bathroom. A shock shoots through my veins when I find blood between my legs, a pool of it freshly staining my white cotton underwear. It's a burgundy mark, scented like the Meat Quarry.

I run to my mother's room.

"I'm bleeding," I say, gesturing between the legs, mortified.

"We don't have time for this," my mother says.

She pushes a thick wad of cotton at me.

"Figure it out," she says. "And you better watch out. Things are going to start changing for you now."

In the bathroom, I mop the blood between my legs. I shove the cotton in the hole where I think it should go.

Outside, through the window, I can see my brother pushing meat toward the house, slick and red as wet roses.

- The earliest recorded mention of the menstrual pad was in the 10th century
- Hypatia, an Egyptian philosopher, astronomer, and mathematician, was said to have thrown one of her used menstrual rags at an admirer in an attempt to discourage him
- The first disposable menstrual pads evolved from a Benjamin Franklin invention created to help stop wounded soldiers from bleeding
- Rags, soil, and mud are used for collecting menstrual flow by women in developing countries who cannot afford disposable pads or tampons

I CALL SOPHIA, MY ANGER DISSOLVED into need.

"I'm sorry," I say into the phone. "I shouldn't have blamed it on you. The words on my desk, I mean."

"I'd never do that to you," Sophia says.

And just like that, we're made up.

"Something happened," I say.

"Come over," Sophia says.

AT SOPHIA'S HOUSE, WE HIDE IN HER room. I whisper it to her.

"I bled this morning."

"No! You got it first?"

I nod. The cotton is still thick between my legs.

"What does it feel like?"

"It's like being hurt, but the blood never stops."

"I missed you," Sophia says. "My mom has been treating me like shit."

"I missed you too," I say. "I think Jarred might like me again."

THAT NIGHT, I BLEED THROUGH THE cotton and through my clothes. I wake drenched in the wetness of my own blood, the white of the mattress ruined.

DAYS LATER, JARRED KISSES ME IN THE empty hallway between classes. He presses his face hard against mine.

"I think I like you," he says.

His mouth tastes like salt and metal. I touch his hair and it is like touching a holy monument. I go quiet from the glow of it. Below, I am still bleeding, red, redder, reddest, bleeding and kissing.

- Only the macaque monkey has a period similar to a woman's, with a cycle that lasts for 29 days
- The body releases roughly three tablespoons of blood during a regular menstrual cycle
- Before the invention of artificial lighting, it is believed women only menstruated during the new moon

EACH SPRING, THE MEAT BLOOMS. THIS year, the harvest is huge, wild, flesh bursting out from the walls of the quarry. The people in town complain about the great stench.

"Goddamn," my father says at dinner. He wipes red dirt from his forehead.

"You're telling me," my brother says.

They're both lean from working the land so hard, each day the meat harvest doubled. We go to town twice each week now, sell it all.

"Proud of my men," my mother says.

"I want to help in the Meat Quarry," I say.

My mother's mouth clenches like a fist.

"What did you say?" my father asks.

"I want to help," I say again. "I'm ready."

My brother lets out a laugh.

"You wouldn't make it one day out there," he says. "Not with that damn knot."

"Now, now," my father says. "Let's not pretend we couldn't use the help."

He clears his throat.

"One day," he says. "You have one day in the quarry."

WE RIDE OUT TO THE MEAT QUARRY IN the early morning sun. I sit next to my father, my brother in the backseat.

I am wearing work clothes: Overalls, boots, busted t-shirt.

"Now listen," my father says. "Don't be hard on yourself today. Just do your best."

"I will," I say.

"You also have to be careful out there," my father says. "Helmet, all right? No bullshit."

He passes me a thermos of coffee and I take a swig.

"Your mother is pissed as hell," he says with a laugh.

There are knives in the coffee, but I gulp it down.

"Oh well," I say. "I'm tired of cleaning that damn house."

My father lets out a howl.

"Oh, you're honest today?" he asks.

I nod vigorously and look out the window as if his laughter doesn't light me up inside, as if it isn't a prize, as if it isn't a thousand golden coins raining down on me.

ONCE WE ARRIVE, MY FATHER PLOPS AN orange helmet on my head. It has a light on the front that makes the meat bright wherever I turn my head. We each grab a silver bucket.

"No fucking funny stuff," my brother says. "We don't need you collapsing this whole damn vein."

We follow the small set of silver tracks deeper into the still-dark quarry and take a left toward the new deposit my brother found. The walkways get smaller and smaller around our bodies, the walls bursting with flesh.

We reach the smallest part of the quarry, a place we have to kneel to enter. An empty silver cart waits nearby on the tracks.

The meat around us is the perfect color for harvest. The walls are so swollen they are almost touching, as if we are kneeling in the corridors of a giant heart.

"Watch us first, then we'll let you try," my father calls.

My father and brother bring their hands to the walls and begin to tug out large wet chunks.

"The bigger the chunks, the more money we can get for them raw," my father explains. "So, you can't be scared to go deep."

My brother does just what he says: He reaches elbow deep into the wall and pulls, removing a boulder-sized chunk of meat from the quarry. He lugs it over to the cart, stumbling a bit from the weight of it.

"See there? That's a big haul."

"There's a reason they say I'm the best."

"You're up, Cassie," my father says.

The wall of meat shimmers beneath the light on my helmet. I pull my arms back and sink them deep into the red wetness of the flesh. The thick scent of blood rises up, fills my mouth and my nostrils until I gag.

"Now, keep strong," my father whispers. "Grip what you can and pull."

I grip the meat strong and pull back with my whole weight, knot and all. The meat sucks at my arms, but I pull harder. Finally, it comes loose, a bigger chunk than what my brother pulled.

My father lets out a yelp.

"Well would you look at that! A natural!"

I keep going, digging my arms into the wall, hearing that familiar wet suck sound, pulling hard. Over and over again, I fill the carts alongside my father and my brother.

By the end of the day, the wall of the quarry is dug out good. Blood coats my skin and my hair and my face and my clothes. We ride home like soldiers from a red war, exhilarated, exhausted, muscles screaming.

"What a fine haul," my father says. "Fine haul."

IT IS MY BIRTHDAY. MY RIBS HAVE BEGUN to show above the knot.

All morning, I imagine: Frosting, butter, perfectly sculpted sugar flowers.

In the kitchen, my family rings the table. There is a small pile of gifts, wrapped in silver.

"HAPPY BIRTHDAY!" everyone sings.

For a moment, briefly, joy.

I take a seat and open the gifts: New dress, new pearls, a book, a journal.

"Now," my mother says. "It is time for your treat."

My body is ready. I will gorge on it, get wild on sugar, explode into a pile of young confetti.

My mother comes back from the kitchen holding a silver tray. She holds the tray so high I cannot see over it, even though I strain.

"Happy Birthday!" she cheers. "All for you!"

A small watering begins in the corners of my mouth as she lowers the tray.

Disappointment busts black through my veins. Stacks of black rocks are shaped like a three-layer cake. No frosting, no sugar, just granite from the ground, that familiar red glisten.

THE NEXT DAY, MY FATHER PRESSES A KEY into my palm.

"Once a week," he says. "You can come harvest."

A real smile comes to my face.

"Ah! So, she does smile," he teases.

And so, it begins: Each week, I spend one day in the quarry, tearing the meat from the walls.

JARRED COMES TO THE HOUSE TO CALL on me.

"May I take Cassie on a walk?" he asks my father on the front porch.

"Better you than me," my father jokes.

Jarred doesn't laugh.

"Cassie, you have a visitor," my father calls up.

WE TAKE THE PATH AWAY FROM THE RED barn, which recedes like an old heart in the distance. My body quickens around him, my pulse, the breath, the lungs trying to catch air.

"Let's sit next to the tree," he says.

I keep my body near his, in case he is ready to touch me.

"I rode my bike to your house," he says.

"That's a long way."

"Took an hour."

I want his words to stop and his hands to move. I always imagine it, this touching, the knee between the legs, the sweet pink sensation, a candy.

"That's a long time," I say.

Then I smash my mouth onto his, taste the salty metal again, the cut of his braces through his lips to mine. He puts his hands on my shoulders and we keep our mouths pressed like that, motionless, holding our breath. Then he pulls away.

"Can I touch you?" he asks.

I nod.

He puts his mouth on mine and we hold our mouths together again and his hands move up my legs, up past the hem of my black dress. I feel dizzy from wanting more, from his still mouth, from his hands. He keeps going. I hold my breath as he moves his hand up to my knot.

"I don't—"

"Shhh," he says.

He puts his mouth on my neck, fingers reaching my knot and caressing it, making me tremble. His hands go greedy, running over the knot, digging into the crevices, gripping the curves of it.

"You're hurting me," I say, panic rising in my throat.

"Good," he says, pressing harder against me, pushing my body into the grass, sliding on top of me, grabbing the knot with both hands now.

He shoves my dress up so my knot and underwear are exposed in the sun. He looks down at me in disgust.

"Look at you," he hisses. "You're fucking gross."

"But I tho—"

"I just wanted to see it for myself," he says.

I start to pull my dress down.

"Leave it," he grunts.

He stands up and spits on the ground next to me.

"Fucking freak," he mutters.

My mouth burns where he kissed me. I watch his back recede into the distance.

I stay that way for hours, until the sun sets, until it is dark, until it is too cold to stay how he left me. I stand up, let my dress fall down, walk home slow.

THE QUARRY MAKES ME STRONGER. THE fat falls from my body, the knot gets smaller. I can see new muscles in my legs and arms. I work fast as my brother, become the slick machine. Meat smears on me like blood on a warrior.

At night, my mother runs her finger over my cheekbones.

"Well, would you look at this," she says. "Sharp as a knife by now."

Little by little, the lemons fall away. The blood turns black beneath my fingernails, which no longer sting. I stand tall when I haul the meat, just like my father, just like my brother.

ONE DAY, I COME HOME FROM THE MEAT Quarry to find my mother alone in her bedroom, surrounded by lemons. There are lemons on the bed, lemons on the chair, lemons on the nightstand.

"Just letting them ripen," she says.

A wince crosses her face and she doubles over in the afternoon light.

"What's wrong?" I ask.

"My knot, it's been hurting," she says. "Just something that comes with age."

I move closer to her and put a hand on her shoulder. She lets out another strange laugh, her white teeth radiating, pain warping her face again.

EACH NEW MOON, I BLEED BETWEEN THE legs like an animal. I am tethered to the sky. I bow my head to the cycle, dip my fingers into the red mess between my legs.

JARRED DOESN'T SPEAK TO ME NOW. SOME days, I want his body on me more than others. Some days, I want his body on mine so badly I could scream into the sky. But we never say a word. I remember his spit in the dirt, a clear gem on the ground that sank into the soil, disappeared.

THE SUN GETS BRIGHTER, THE SUMMER days hotter and longer. I work the quarry, dig in the field for strange rocks, knife tops, bones.

In my palm, I hold the bleached summer bones of a small bird. When I shift my fingers, the bones touch, make a soft hollow sound. I keep the bones near me after that, like a totem. They stay on my nightstand where I can touch them when the bad feelings come down.

ONE DAY, I FIND THE CARCASS OF A DEER. I stare down into its open dead eye, which reflects the world around us in a glistening blue.

The deer's belly is split open and its organs spill out: Winding pink intestines next to a deep red heart next to an opaque stomach like a big hideous pearl on the green grass. A sad electricity shoots through me. I memorize the insides, the blood on the fur, in the wide eye.

JARRED COMES TO ME IN THE AFTER-noon, by the lockers.

"I want to see you again," he says.

My brain swells, goes dizzy and wild with the thought of it.

"Me?" I ask.

"Yes, you. Fucking freak," he says, but this time he cracks a smile like he won't spit.

"When?"

"After school. I'll walk you."

I spend the rest of the day in a haze imagining it: His mouth on mine, his body near mine, his hands on me. The hours ache by. I stare up at the clock and urge it forward.

I WALK TOWARD MY HOUSE WITH JARRED.

"I'm sorry about last time," he says.

I nod, unsure what comes next.

We move quietly over the land. The heat from his body makes me quiet until my house comes into view.

"No one is home until six…" I say.

We sit on the couch and stare at the wall. The air is electric. I am waiting for something to happen and then it does, then it is his mouth on mine again, this time without the metal, still salt, this time his tongue against mine, a new sensation, our tongues. I go ravenous, an animal, heat growing between our bodies.

He peels off my dress and runs his hands up the knot. He slides his hands up to my breasts, cups them through my bra.

"Take it off," he hisses, and I do, then there is nothing between our skin, his hands on my nipples, then his mouth, a fire.

He snakes his hand down to my jeans. The zipper parts and his hand is between my legs, his fingers finding the thicket of hair there then stopping cold.

"Jesus, you're hairy," he mutters. "You don't shave?"

I flush red and go motionless.

"Shave?"

"Down there, shave," he says. "Girls are supposed to shave that."

He takes his hand from my pants.

"Jesus, what's wrong with you?" he asks.

I open my mouth to tell him I am working with the doctors to get the knot removed. I want to give him hope for our future, but the words won't come out.

There is a series of sounds in succession: His receding footsteps, the front door opening then slamming, then he's gone.

THE SUN SETS AS I CROSS THE FIELDS, SKY dripping sherbet colors: Light yellow, twilight orange, deep pink.

At the entrance, I put on my helmet, cast the light.

Deep in the quarry, I take the left. I let the walls close in on me, down into the deepest section.

Rage puts me in motion: I claw at the walls with my hands, bury my arms in the meat. I rip the flesh from the walls, screaming and sobbing against the red.

AT BREAKFAST THE NEXT MORNING, WE sit quietly until my father mentions it.

"Some animal got at the Meat Quarry last night," he says. "Strange, because I know I locked it up."

The bloody clothes are in the hamper. How long until someone finds me out? A strange calmness has entered my veins since the meat screaming. Nothing can shake me now.

"I wonder what kind of animal it was," I say.

"No telling, but it might've been a wolf. That's how much damage was done."

I slide a piece of rock into my mouth to hide my smile.

"I have to say, the economy isn't holding strong," my father says. "Some troubling signs in the paper lately."

"Like what?" my mother asks.

"Unstable dollar, more meat than usual available," my father says. "Plus, people are eating more spinach these days, less meat. At least, that's what the reports are saying."

All day long, I hum it to myself:

I am the wolf, I am the wolf, I am the wolf.

"HAVE YOU EVER SHAVED?" I ASK SOPHIA.

We're sitting in her bathroom after school. She has started wearing red lipstick.

"Of course," Sophia says. "How else can you show yourself to men?"

"How did you learn to do it?"

Sophia looks at me with pity and disgust.

"You're not shaving? Didn't your mom show you?"

I shake my head.

Sophia pulls a razor from a drawer and presses it into my palm.

"Figure it out, Cassie. Jesus Christ."

I CLIMB INTO THE WHITE PORCELAIN bathtub with Sophia's razor. I lather myself up good in the hot water, white soap bubbling all around me.

I bring the razor to the softest skin there and guide it over me, specks of thick hair falling with the soap to the tub floor. I move slowly, carefully, delicately.

My knot shifts me and I slip, the razor slicing the skin between my legs, blood dripping from the mouth of the wound onto the porcelain.

MY MOTHER EYES ME AT BREAKFAST. Today, she is kind, friendly.

"I miss you," she says. "It feels like we're just not close anymore."

"I know!" I say. "I've just been so busy with school and the Meat Quarry."

"She's getting really good," my brother says.

"Look how beautiful you are now," my mother says.

She reaches across the table to run a hand over my cheek.

"Look at your lips," she whispers. "I wish I had lips."

IT IS MY BROTHER'S BIRTHDAY. I MAKE the cake: I crack eggs, whip a perfect white frosting.

We crowd around the table and sing the song.

"You all sound terrible," he says.

My mother hits his arm. He forks cake into his mouth.

In the low, low light, across the table, I love him. I want to say it, but it gets trapped in my throat, a motionless red lump, worthless as a heart.

"I SHAVED," I WHISPER AT JARRED WHEN he passes me in the hall.

I watch the back of his head for a reaction. His body doesn't change, his shoulders don't tense, he doesn't flinch. It's as if no one has spoken, as if I am a ghost.

Later, a note on my desk:

Let me walk you home today.

Heat flushes: Our mouths together again, the skin beneath my skin, his skin above my skin, the warmth, the warmth a new small sun between the legs.

AFTER SCHOOL, WE WANDER THE ACRES.

"I like it when you listen to me," Jarred says.

"I want to show you something," I say. "Have you seen the Meat Quarry?"

"No," he says. "Where's that?"

"Just out this way," I say.

I guide him down the road until we reach the gate.

I slide my key into the lock until it clicks. He follows me inside, his eyes flicking over the flesh walls.

"What is this place?" he asks.

"The Meat Quarry. My brother and father discovered it. It's ours."

"What do you do down here?"

"This is where we harvest the meat."

"Weird," he says. "Smells like hell."

"It's my favorite place."

"Come here."

I walk to him, body more electric. He shoves his mouth against mine. It's rough, the way he does it this time, his teeth against my lips and tongue, his hand on the side of my face.

He lets out a low moan and slides his hand up my skirt, past my underwear, his fingers on my bare skin.

"Good, good," he says.

The heat between my legs grows, glows, turns white. He presses me back against the meat, the walls soaking blood into my back and hair. I don't mind, I tell myself *I don't mind.*

He slides my dress from my shoulder, a mouth to a breast, his hands roving over my knot, then his fingers finding the space between my legs and pressing inside of me so deeply that it hurts.

I let out a small cry and he smiles.

"Too much?" he asks.

I nod.

"Oh well," he says. He wraps his teeth around my earlobe and shoves his fingers in deeper.

Panic begins in my chest. I push his shoulders back, away from me. He steps back to peel his shirt off, then he's on me again, his skin against mine, the blood from the wall soaking me.

"Oh, no," he says. "We've come all this way."

I hear the mouth of the zipper, and the same scent from the classroom comes back to me, the scent of his private skin, the pink of him, the sound of his hand against himself. He covers my mouth with his and yanks my underwear to the side. I start to shriek into his mouth. It must sound like a moan.

"Oh, fuck yes," he mutters.

It happens so fast I don't know what it is, but then he is inside of me, the hardness of him, the tearing of my body, a strange harsh heat searing between my legs.

He moves against me fast and hard, a terrible friction, faster and faster, until he moans like before, shudders like before, fills me with another heat, and collapses against my body.

"Wasn't that nice?" he murmurs. "You liked that, didn't you?"

I stare up at the red quarry in the afternoon light, wet faced, numb, chest empty.

VISION

After school, we wander The Acres.

"I like it when you listen to me," Jarred says.

"I want to show you something," I say. "Have you seen the Meat Quarry?"

"No," he says. "Where's that?"

"Just out this way," I say.

I guide him down the road until we reach the gate.

I slide my key into the lock until it clicks. He follows me inside, his eyes flicking over the flesh walls.

"What is this place?" he asks.

"The Meat Quarry. My brother and father discovered it. It's ours."

"What do you do down here?"

"This is where we harvest the meat."

"Weird," he says. "Smells like hell."

"It's my favorite place."

"Come here."

I walk to him, body more electric. He shoves his mouth against mine. It's rough, the way he does it this time, his teeth against my lips and tongue, his hand on the side of my face, tender.

"I really like you," he says. "I think about you all the time."

"I like you too," I say.

He puts his mouth back on mine. I run my hands through his wild hair, over his chest beneath his worn t-shirt. He lets out a low moan and slides his hand up my skirt, past my underwear, his fingers on my bare skin.

We slide to the ground. I can feel him hard against my leg. The heat between my legs grows, glows, turns white. He presses his mouth into my hair.

I pull back and stare deep into his eyes. He keeps going, sliding my dress from my shoulder, then his mouth to my breast, his hands keep roving, running over my knot.

"Can I touch you?" he asks.

I nod and he does, gently, lightly sliding a finger into me. He puts his mouth back on mine and I keep my body close to him, close to his warmth.

I hear the mouth of the zipper, and the same scent from the classroom comes back to me, the scent of his private skin, the pink of him, the sound of his hand against himself.

"Is this OK?" he asks.

I nod. He moves slowly, gently, staring deep into my eyes in the dimming lavender sunset against the red quarry swells as he sinks into me, my breath catching from the pain and pleasure of it, the early hint of love between us.

THE NEXT MORNING BRINGS THE NUMB sun. The air is warm, summer heat preparing for the day. I cannot bring my body out of bed.

"I'm sick," I explain to my mother.

"Poor thing," she says, rubbing my forehead. "You look bloodless. Let me take care of you."

She piles the bedside table with soup, medicine, tissues, leftover cake. It all stays untouched. I am still covered in his terrible fingers, his teeth, his tongue, his saliva my new skin.

I curl into myself, sleep when the ache gets too big to breathe.

"WHAT IS WRONG WITH YOU?" MY mother asks. "You don't harvest anymore."

"It's boring. Who cares about meat? Who?" I snap.

"Better you're here cleaning anyway, where you belong."

My hands are full of lemons. I feel covered in ash.

"CAN I SEE YOU AGAIN?" JARRED ASKS IN the hall at school, weeks later, weeks after not speaking, not making eye contact.

His mouth keeps moving, but I cannot hear a sound. The world has gone blank. There is no blood left in me.

I DREAM OF THE MEAT QUARRY, MY BODY pressed deep into the red again. I writhe in the meat and rip at the walls, harvesting faster than ever, screaming.

PAIN NUMBS THE SKIN, THE COLORS, THE dazzle of the world. The moon no longer speaks to me. I become the pale void, an empty pink shell.

PART II

I RENT A SMALL APARTMENT FAR FROM The Acres, distant from the Meat Quarry, in the belly of the city. Each month, I send in the rent. The apartment is mine that way: I pay to keep my body there at night.

Each morning, I read the jobs section of the newspaper, black print fingers streaking my face and the white walls of the apartment. The headlines read:

LEGAL CLERK NEEDED

ODD JOB EXPERT DESIRED

POSITION VACANT

CAREER OPPORTUNITY

WANTED: PASSIONATE TYPIST

LET ME TELL YOU HOW THE CITY FEELS to me: It is an orchestra of rusting metal, heaving trucks and sharp silver buildings, full of bodies, faces, color, electricity.

On the small squares of grass, there are small piles of dog shit. In each concrete corner, there is a small pool of urine. On the walls, there are electric scrawls of graffiti in a language I do not know.

At night, the skyline shoots out pinpricks of light and I am in awe. In the morning, I get trash caught on my ankles, greased Styrofoam making its sound against my skin. Even that is beautiful.

ON THE STREETS, I BLUR INTO THE population. I mix into the faces.

Here, no one notices the knot unless they get too close. They don't even realize there is a pool of sweat in the largest crevice, into which one might toss a very small pebble, causing ripples.

"Got any change?" a man screams from a wheelchair.

His mouth hangs open, a single tooth protruding from the red of his collapsing gums.

"This world is pain!" screams a woman next to him.

Her eyes are bloodshot, watery, weary.

I slide a gold coin into each of their cups.

"What the fuck you looking at?" screams the woman. "Get moving, bitch! This isn't a movie!"

I disappear quick, knot throbbing hard, into the smear of the city's faces.

- The first cities were built roughly 11,000 years ago
- Agriculture, slaughter, and farming are believed to be a prerequisite for cities; consistent food supplies made it easier for people to live in one place
- Cities reduced transport costs for goods by bringing large populations into one location

MY APARTMENT IS UP A WIDE FLIGHT OF stairs. It is on the second floor, a small one bedroom with wide windows, dark wooden floors, white walls, a tiny kitchen. It is like the house at The Acres in this way.

I don't have much: My clothes and books, a few rocks which glisten in the sun.

Outside, a constant chorus of noise: Breaking glass, trash trucks, arguments, a baby sobbing out all the tragedies of the world through its wailing.

THE AD I CHOOSE FROM THE PAPER SAYS:

> **WANTED: PASSIONATE TYPIST**
>
> Can you type quickly and with passion? We want to add you to our vibrant, culturally dynamic office. We offer competitive salary, free water, and a positive workplace. To apply, please send a photograph from the neck up.

"AND HOW WOULD YOU CONTRIBUTE TO the culture here in addition to typing up my daily notes?" the man in the suit asks.

The bald sheen of his head shines through several slicked, thin hairs. His skin is covered in strange red freckles, a blotching which travels beneath collar and shirt sleeve. The dead skin of his face is caught on his eye glasses, which are smeared with the thin yellow grease of his fingers and cheeks.

A stack of papers sits on his desk, many folders, an old mug of coffee. I picture myself typing up the notes every single day. Then, I picture my fingers in the brown sludge ringing his coffee mug, smearing it across my face like war paint.

"I would smile pretty frequently," I say, smiling. "I bring a positive energy to the workplace."

"Excellent," he says. "We don't appreciate frowning here."

"Absolutely," I nod and smile.

"And as for your… condition?" he asks. He uses his eyes to gesture to my knot. "Are you with child?"

"Oh no, no. It's just a knot. It won't stop me from doing my job," I explain. "It's just how I look."

"Fantastic. We like to give people opportunities," he explains. "I believe in rewarding a hard worker, no matter the ah… circumstances."

I shake his hand over the desk.

IN THE GROCERY STORE, THE LIGHTS ARE dazzling, the heads of the vegetables wanting for eyes. I move among the foods like a gone woman, hypnotized. I pile the cart high and trance my way to the meat counter.

"Hello," says a man in a white coat.

"Hello, I'll have some meat."

"Well, yeah. What kind?"

He gestures at the spread below the glass. The meats are strange and new: Coiled like organs, too pink, chopped to bits, too full of white rivers of fat. None of the meats make sense here.

"I don't… I don't know."

"Lady, nobody here has this much time to kill."

My eyes finally land on the red meat I know, huge round hunks of it like from the earth. I imagine my father pulling this meat from the quarry, cleaning it, and selling it. I imagine the meat traveling here to meet me through a series of silver trains and black trucks.

"That one," I say, gesturing.

"How much?"

"Two pounds."

"It's your world, lady, I'm just living in it."

"Miss, you want to hurry up already?" calls a man from the line which has grown behind me.

His eyes are on the back of my neck, I feel them like the points of knives.

"It's not like I don't know my meats!" I exclaim to the large back of the meat man, to anyone who might be listening.

SOPHIA CALLS AND HER VOICE MAKES ME homesick. She lives in an apartment too, in our hometown, back near The Acres.

"It's closer to the stores and the men," she says. "I did meet someone new."

"What do you mean?" I ask.

"I met a man. He's really wonderful," she says.

The word *wonderful* is a foreign land.

"That's great," I say. "What is it like?"

"It's hard to describe it. It's beautiful. I never thought I'd be so deeply understood and fully completed as a human as I am now with Doug. How's the city?"

"That's great," I say. "The city is just incredible."

The lie strains through my teeth.

EACH MORNING, I YANK THE STRAY HAIRS from my face, brush my teeth, apply my makeup.

Then I put on the costume for work: Black pants, white blouse, green cardigan, low-heeled black shoes.

Before I leave, I put in my false heart, which sits in front of my regular heart. The false heart is made of thin red plastic and covers my real heart, quiets the beating, an extra protection.

I walk slowly to the office. I have a short daydream about my body back home, in bed, in the warmth and sheets. The vision washes over me like a drug, what a pleasant pleasure just to imagine it.

AT MY DESK, I TYPE THE BALD MAN'S notes. My fingers buzz across the keyboard, letters kicked up like the black wings of crushed bugs.

"My god, you're fast," the boss says.

"Thank you," I say.

"You're like a goddamn automatic weapon," he says. "What did you do this weekend?"

I go clammy, a bit of sweat on the brow, in the palms, beneath the arms.

"Nothing much," I say.

A deep silence stands between us, my mouth a closed shell I pry open.

"...And you?" I tack on.

"Oh, you know, took the old boat out, a few rounds of golf, a nice steak."

"That sounds lovely," I say.

He offers a wink through his greasy glasses, upon which I note the specific swirls of his fingerprints.

"You keep typing that fast, that could be your life someday," he says.

I picture it: My mouth full of steak, the steak in my mouth, the steak between my teeth, strings of fat in the molars, my jaw aching from always chewing, chewing and swallowing until I'm so full that my throat sews itself shut.

- Most workers spend 1,896 hours per year at the office
- The average office worker spends 50 minutes per day looking for lost files
- *Stewardesses* is one of the longest words typed with only the left hand
- A typist's fingers travel 12.6 miles on the average work day

ON CERTAIN DAYS, WHAT HAPPENED IN the Meat Quarry rises up from my belly and seizes my heart.

I can feel his hands on me.

I can feel my body pressed into the red.

Wasn't that nice? You liked that, didn't you?

I shove those feelings back down into the knot.

VISION

On Wednesdays, Jarred meets me halfway between our offices, on the concrete. His eyes glint pleasant as metal. Joy rises up in my chest to see him, to slide my hand into his.

"How was your day?" he asks.

"I typed the president's notes again," I say. "How was your day?"

"I worked on the computers," he says. "The usual."

We wander the blocks, lazy-legged. The sun seems to be in our favor, washing over our arms, a false summer. The beast in my heart rests, calm, fangs in. A slow spool of silver thread unwinds in my bloodstream, a shiver of pleasure.

At the restaurant, we order our favorite: Two burgers, fries. I watch his mouth split and bite into the meat, and it is as beautiful as a painting, as beautiful as an oil painting, as beautiful as anything I have ever seen.

THE WOMEN IN THE CITY WEAR HIGH heels and sharp suits. Their bodies are lithe. It seems only skin is stretched over their bones, muscle removed.

"What would you like today?" asks the woman in white inside the silver lunch truck. Her mouth is puckered, a glare to her eyes. I've taken too long again.

"What did she have?"

I point to the city woman standing a few feet away. She's pencil-thin, an arrow, long hair highlighted to perfection. My loose clothes blow around on me. I am a linen line in the wind.

"A fucking salad, come on."

"I'll have a salad."

I watch her while I eat, lettuce in my mouth, between the teeth. I watch the way her clothes tuck around her wired body, her eyes on the horizon, looking into a future I cannot see.

THERE IS NOTHING TO IT, THE MOTIONS, I go through them each day.

I build a new life out of minutes filled with small actions, my distraction techniques:

WASHING HAIR

SHAVING BODY

STARING THROUGH WINDOW

EATING

MASTURBATING

SLEEPING

I repeat and I repeat and I repeat. I inch toward death.

EACH NIGHT AT HOME, I WASH OFF THE mask. Then, I place the false heart in a small black box on the dresser.

After, I make a simple dinner: Chicken, starch, vegetable. The meat tastes gray in my mouth.

The silence of the apartment swells. Later, in bed, my mind churns, my organs grind against each other, a swarm of bees thrum through my veins until I slide my hand between my legs, until the sweet pink rush before I sleep.

SOPHIA CALLS.

"We're in love," she says.

I picture love: They must be next to each other in bed. They must be feeding each other small cakes. They are definitely fucking constantly. They must be warm.

Outside, the city starts a cold rain. I curl into bed alone.

MY DREAMS ESCALATE IN THEIR strangeness. I dream of the Meat Quarry with a broken gate.

I wander in deep, until I find my family, sitting on the ground, mouths covered in red, filled with meat, teeth pink, roaring with laughter, tears streaming from their eyes.

"There you are!" my father booms. "We've been waiting!"

In the dream, I can sense Jarred at the periphery of the quarry, the long black shadow of his danger.

I wake sandy-mouthed, dehydrated, safe, alone.

EACH FRIDAY, THE BOSS CARRIES A SMALL black velvet pouch. This is called PAY DAY and it is marked on the calendar with a single exclamation point.

"Good job again this week," he says. "Here's what makes the world go 'round, am I right?"

He gives me a wink.

"The world goes 'round," I say.

The pouch settles on my desk with a thud. I can hear the weight of it. I open it slowly, pour the golden coins into my hand.

I count the coins, one by one, into my palm where they glint briefly in the sun. Soon enough the coins are gone, out into the open mouths of debt and food.

ON WEEKENDS, I FALL BACK INTO OLD routines. Mid-day, I realize I am washing the white walls of my apartment with lemons.

Then I shower, wash the triangle of hair between my legs, scrub my body with fine-grit salts until my skin screams.

Later in the grocery store, I speak like a pro at the meat counter:

"I'll have a steak, please."

Then I put the steak in the cart. I push the cart to the checkout lane and pay for it.

At home: Marinate, temperature check, make the flesh good and cooked, then devour the territory.

VISION

I don't ask for much at home. It is silent there. I light three candles, then I stare at the walls while the hours pass.

On the walls, I keep a calendar. Here, I monitor my emotional states. Today, for instance, I write down EVACUATED because I don't feel myself in my body. Instead, I feel like a glistening container waiting to be filled with an event or a love. Each morning in the mirror, I chant the phrase, "I am someone waiting for something to happen."

Sometimes, I play a record. Sometimes, I read a book.

Within the pages of the book are photographs of craters in the earth taken from space. Often, the craters look like scars on the human skin of land. When a crater hits earth, debris is released which can pollute the air, or even block the sun. It is important to learn one fact each day to keep the mind sharp.

Always, I am standing outside of myself while I watch my other self complete these tasks. I report back with updates: We are eating chicken. We are sharpening our minds. We are expanding our skill sets. One day, someone will happen upon us and love us genuinely and truly for these motions.

BEFORE BED, MY PHONE RINGS, THEN MY mother's voice.

"How are you? How is the big city treating you?"

"Great! Fine, really. The weather is great. How is it back home?"

"Oh, you know, just the way it always is. Boring! And you know your father, out in the damn Meat Quarry. Your brother, too. I might as well not even exist!"

"That's not true," I force myself to say.

"Oh, you know how the boys are. I will say, business has slowed down, so they are working overtime to make up for it."

"Why is it slowing down?"

"You know, too many people selling the same thing. Can't transport the meat as fast as some others. What about you? Any men in the picture?"

"Nothing serious. How is your knot feeling?"

A small silence.

"It's been acting up," she says. "You know how it is. It comes with time."

The pain she hides radiates through her voice. I can feel it coming for me. I can feel it breathing down my neck, my terrible ancestor.

IN THE BAR, BOTTLES LINE THE MIR- rored walls. I catch a glimpse of my eyes between their necks.

A man sits next to me. His nose is sharp, his eyes are deep green, his hair brown. His smell is my father's same smell: sour, sweet, a thin layer of meat at the base of it.

"Hello," I say.

"Hey there. You come here often?" he asks.

"No, I usually just stay home and cry in bed," I say.

He lets out a laugh.

"What do you do?"

"I type the company notes every day," I say. "What do you do?"

"I'm a law man," he says. "I deal with the laws."

"Oh."

"Does that impress you?"

"I guess."

He reaches into his pocket and pulls out a handful of gold coins. He sits them on the bar. I smell him again, that deep smell, and I want his hands on me.

"Does it now?"

"Sure," I say.

His hand finds my leg and squeezes. I let it happen, I want it to happen, I follow that feeling with him, out into the night, then into my apartment.

IN THE DIM LIGHT OF MY SMALL KITCHEN, he puts his hands on my shoulders. I keep my mouth on him. He tastes sharp.

"You smell so good," he says into my skin, into my shoulder. His hands slide down my arms to my waist, where they discover my knot.

"Wha…" he asks.

"Oh, it's just… I was born with it."

"What the hell is it?" he asks, his fingers digging into the curves.

"It's just this thing… my mother has it too, it's a knot…"

"Your body is a knot?"

"Well just… my stomach, yes…"

"Show it to me, right now."

I step back and lift my dress slowly, until his eyes can take it all in, my warped body.

"Look, you're great. You are. But I don't… I don't think I can do this," he mutters. "This isn't for me."

I drop my dress back down over the knot. I nod.

"It's OK, I understand."

A succession of sounds: Doors opening and closing, the car engine starting, tires kicking up loose rock from the asphalt, then the silence again, always only silence for me.

"YOU WERE LATE THIS MORNING," THE boss says, standing over my desk. "I came looking for you and couldn't find you."

My hair is dirty. There are dirty half-moons beneath my fingernails. I notice the faint scent of filth wafting from between my legs. My blood is sand in the veins.

"I'm sorry," I say. "I overslept."

"Work late," he says. "Don't let it happen again."

A brief hallucination: I smash the windows out, scream until the metal cabinets collapse, until the fluorescent lights rain down on my face in a shatter of glass, blood streaking my face. Then I leave early.

Instead, I put my head down. I work.

At lunch, I eat a hamburger, let the clear pink juice run down my lips like an animal. The leftover liquor in my stomach makes the food expand, my knot thick with bloat.

Later, I sit at my desk, a good worker until the sun sets, until the clock's hands touch a certain number, until it is time to pack up, walk back to the bar.

SOPHIA CALLS AGAIN WITH BIGGER NEWS.

"I'm pregnant!" she says.

My vision gets small.

"That's beautiful," I machine into the line. "When are you due?"

IN A DREAM, MY ABDOMEN SWELLS AND swells. Yet I do not give birth. I rub my hand over my distended belly and listen for the sounds of child. There is nothing.

"We can't tell what's wrong," the dream doctors say. "We just don't understand this baby."

This goes on for months until I get fed up. I make an incision in my own belly. It barely hurts. I part the wound to find my child, but there are only bright white worms, eyeless, writhing.

AN ACHE BEGINS IN MY KNOT. THE LAN-guage of pain means nothing: Do I mean a cramp? Is it a fire? Is an ache a roar?

I look for cures. I rub the knot with Epsom salts. I attempt a self-massage. I drench myself in expensive healing oils.

SPECIAL HEALING OILS

Created under a full moon and with the use of crystals, this series of oils will realign your chakras and remove pain from the body. These claims have not been validated by the FDA.

The hurt persists beneath the oils. I count the rhythm of the pangs on the walk to work.

My mind starts to unravel. The scenery warps. The world flattens around me. The busy street I'm standing on is just a painting, a canvas I could punch my fist through.

THE BREAK ROOM AT WORK IS PAINTED orange. The refrigerator is filthy white from our fingerprints. A low light buzzes above my head. I spoon my soup into my mouth, split pea green between the lips.

"Whatcha got there?" asks Brenda.

The pain still trembles through my knot, a pain Brenda cannot see or comprehend. Brenda has chopped brown bangs, watery brown eyes. Her shirt hangs sloppily over her thin frame. A small barrette holds back her bangs, giving a childlike appearance to her grown body.

"Soup," I say, gesturing to the soup.

"Ooooh," she says. "Soup! What kind?"

This is an attempt at friendship, a forcing, another labor among the current labor.

"I wish I had some soup!" she says, pulling her own lunch from her bag: A sandwich on square white bread with a limp piece of green lettuce between the crusts. She slides the sandwich between her thin lips, takes a bite, then speaks.

"You know, I know a guy who fixes that," she says, her eyes on my torso.

The longer her eyes are on my knot, the brighter my rage glows. I stuff it down into my belly.

"Oh?"

"Yep, he's even been on the local news," she says. "His name is Dr. Richard Richardson."

"Is that right?"

"Mhmm, he's got these special injections to help girls like you. He's a miracle worker. I went to see him for the corns on my feet. He fixed all 12 of 'em, they never came back. He froze them right off!"

I picture a dozen pieces of bad toe skin fluttering to the floor, one by one. She takes a pen from her back pocket and jots the number in black ink on a white napkin, which I jam into my back pocket.

"Thank you."

I wash my bowl in the sink, imagining her awful feet, the awful frozen skin of her toes fluttering to the ground around her, the shed petals of a dead flower.

VISION

A perfect day in early fall: The sky bright and blue with the right style of clouds. I hold Jarred's hand in the art museum, the old works of art looming over us.

There is a painting of bright flowers on a dark background nestled around the skull of a shark.

"And this painting, created in the 1900s, is fucking terrible," he whispers.

My laugh bounces off of the canvas and back at us, an echo.

There is a statue of a woman draped in a snake, holding a mirror up to her own face.

"And this is a sculpture of a stuck-up bitch," he hisses, pinching my side until I laugh.

There is a room made to look like Paris: Pastel walls, long mirrors, dazzling chandeliers. We are sore thumbs in all black, pricks of negative light in the setting.

"I hate this," he whispers.

"It's too perfect," I whisper.

Then, we make it ours: We claw at the pastel walls. We lift the tufted chairs and smash them through the mirrors.

We dance on the shards, weave our bloody fingers together, our mouths meet in the center, over our reflections in the rubble.

THE OFFICE OF DR. RICHARD RICHARDSON is in a squat building with an orange roof. It looks too small next to the rest of the buildings, as if it comes from another time.

The sign with his name is aging, fake gold script that spells *Dr. Richar* and fades off.

Inside, the waiting room is marked by several ferns and stacks of magazines with the bottom corners torn off to hide home addresses.

The blue eyes of the receptionist peer over the high black counter at me.

"And are you Cassie?" she asks.

"That's me."

"Well, that's just great! I just have a few forms for you to fill out here and the doctor will be right with you!"

I take the clipboard to the waiting area. I fill out: Name, Address, Emergency Contact.

On the third page, there is a bold headline over two outlines of a generic female body.

PLEASE CIRCLE WHERE YOU ARE SUFFERING, THEN RATE YOUR SUFFERING ON A SCALE FROM 1-10, WITH 10 BEING THE MOST SUFFERING.

One outline shows her front, with little circles for breasts. The other outline shows the back of her body.

I circle the torso then I circle the torso again. I try to calculate my suffering on a numerical scale, assign a value. What is 10? The hottest sun?

I write the number 7.

"Thank you!" she chirps when I hand her the paperwork. "We'll call for you shortly."

In the waiting room magazines, faded recipes measure out ingredients that combine to make: glazed ham, Jell-O salad, a slick series of shiny tortes.

"Dr. Richardson will see you now!"

I follow her down a short hallway full of fake body sections: Plastic heart, plastic spine, plastic liver, each split to show their arteries, vertebrae, veins.

"And you just put this on, he'll be right with you!" she says, pressing the standard paper gown into my hands.

I strip down and put on the gown, skin pricking beneath in the office cold.

"Cassie!" his voice booms when he steps in. "You decent in here?"

"Yes," I say.

He has the face of a Roman god, but old and tired under the eyes, fatter around the middle.

"I've been reading your paperwork," he says, thumping the pages. "Seems like you're a perfect candidate."

"For what?"

"We'll get to that, but first let's take a look under the hood, shall we?"

"The hood?"

"Why don't you just let me have a look at the knot?"

I lie down slowly. He stands next to me, sliding the gown up, resting it below my breasts, cutting me in half, a magician's trick.

"Well, this is one hell of a knot," he murmurs. "Big guy. May I?"

I nod.

He runs his hands over the knot, fingers probing the crevices, the twists, the turns I've already memorized.

"Good, good, now sit up for me and pull that gown down. Let's talk about our options."

"Options?"

"Well, the techniques have advanced," he says. "I'm the only one in the city who can do it. Some would say it's the forefront of medicine."

My heart begins to open slowly, a tentative flower in early spring. I allow myself one moment to imagine it: My body knotless, normal, free.

"Yes, go on. What is it?"

"Well, it's known as the Sugar Water technique," he says. "It helps loosen the knot through a series of 37 injections to the—"

My heart snaps shut.

"Stop right there."

"Well, just conside—"

"No, thank you, please let me get dressed."

"I can he—"

"I'm getting dressed."

THE HALLWAY IS EMPTY WHEN I LEAVE, the fake organs reversing their order: Plastic liver, plastic spine, plastic heart.

The ride home is dizzying, the city whipping by in a montage: Trucks, buildings, dumpsters, women screaming, business men laughing, sad women, small children, clouds darkening above our heads.

In my empty apartment, I climb into bed and wrap myself around the knot, wait for the storm to come down.

- In the early 1900s, physicians injected gold salts into limbs to reduce the pain of arthritis

- The word *pain* derives from the Old French *peine*, from the Latin *poena* for *penalty*

- Hippocrates wrote frequently about trepanation, a practice wherein doctors would cut holes in the skulls of those in pain to release their suffering

- Plato and Aristotle theorized pain originated outside of the body, descending upon it like a demon

- The Egyptians placed eels over the wounds of patients, noting their shocks could relieve pain symptoms

VISION

A man stands on the black sands. His white robes billow in the breeze. He has a thick brown beard and opaque eyes. He reaches out and takes my hand.

"Come with me," he says.

The beach is so black it could be ink. We are walking through a film negative — white sky, dark sand, foaming white ocean. The bodies of silver fish litter the shore, their translucent bodies shimmering against the dark earth.

Nearby, high mossy cliffs serve as home for flocks of white birds which soar and nest in the craters. At the base of the cliffs, a small black mouth opens in the rock.

"This is where I will cure your problems," he says.

"I only have one problem," I say, gesturing to my abdomen.

"You have more problems than just one," he says. "Many more."

He bends down and moves through the low entrance. I follow him into the belly of the dark cave. A match is struck. He lights one candle, then another, then another, then another, a table of white pillared wax coming into view and casting light.

The walls of the cave look more menacing now that I can see them. In the rock, I can make out the dull scratches of men who have been here before, small etchings of men on fire.

He pulls a box from below the table of candles, then steps toward me.

"Please, sit," he says, gesturing to a big rock.

He places the box next to me and kneels before me. He stares deep into my eyes. The white film of his gaze unnerves me.

"Are you prepared to trust me?" he asks.

I stare into his milky eyes, his wrinkled face. I weigh out my days of pain, my weeks of agony, my years of sadness, my life of walking the earth in this body.

"Yes."

"Then let us begin."

He opens the box slowly. Inside, there is water which refracts the candlelight.

"What is the water for?"

"Ah, my dear, it is not only water."

He opens the lid wider. More light creeps into the box, and I can see bodies slithering beneath the water, slick, scaled. Suddenly, a small face comes into view beneath the surface: two eyes, strange nose, a mouth.

"Eels," he says. "For you."

Another face appears in the water. The two eels keep moving, curving around each other.

"Why eels?"

"They will use their current to help you."

"Current?"

"Yes, their shocks will help you."

"I don't believe you."

"Where is your faith?"

"I don't believe in anything."

"You must believe in something on this earth."

"I don't."

"Please, show me your knot. Let me."

I slide off my dress. There is nothing sexual to it — he does not stare at me and I do not look at him. In the flickering candlelight, my body is a deeper puzzle: the shadows make my curved abdomen stranger, more menacing, the neck of a dark swan curled in on itself.

"Now please, if you will, lie down."

I do as I'm told, the cave dirt pressing against my skin.

He slides on a pair of thick gray gloves and opens the box. He moves quickly and with purpose, seizing one eel and raising it out of the water. The eel writhes in the air between us, wet body glinting.

"Are you ready?" he asks.

I nod and he moves toward me without hesitation. Then the eel is laid over my knot, curling into its crevices.

For a moment, the eel is still, which lets my heart rest for a beat. For a moment a new future flashes into mind: the eel and I living together in harmony, its black body attached to mine, a new knot.

Then shock roars through my body where it touches my skin, the black slime of the eel hot with electricity, the light of it tearing through me, making me bright white, writhing, the pain bigger than any I've ever felt.

When I come to, the man stands over me, gloveless, the eel peeled from my body. There is an extra step in my heartbeat. I run a hand over my knot, which is sore to the touch.

"How do you feel?" he asks.

"The same."

"Well, one more time then," he says before I go under, the dark cave closing its mouth around me.

SOPHIA CALLS AND THE BABY HAS COME. The baby is named Tara. I can hear her gurgling in the background.

"Congratulations," I force my mouth to say. "She sounds beautiful."

ON WEEKENDS, I SIT IN THE SILENCE OF the apartment, staring into the open mouth of each hour, into the ticking clock: No one to touch, no movement of the body, an emptiness opening its inside of me.

I reach over to the gold coins on the bedside table. I stack them next to me in bed like a lover, like armor, I run my hands over them, a safe, warm con.

I slide one into my mouth and suck. The metal makes my teeth ache. I want to swallow it. I want the coins to wind through the knot, filling my belly, my body bursting with wealth.

IN THE CLOTHING STORE, BRIGHT BAN-ners proclaim the sales, the promotions wild, excited. I want to look like the city women: lethal, pointed.

Beneath the fluorescent lights, the same haze from the grocery store returns.

"You need help?" the saleslady asks.

"No, thank you, though."

"When are you due?"

"Due what?"

"Your baby, when are you having your baby?"

"I'm not pregnant."

"I'm sorry, I'm so sorry."

I stand in the racks of clothing, deflated, the empty bodies of women without heads. I move the hangers to the left and the right, I search for a nice color to hide within.

In the fitting room, I slide the new colors over my head. I try on a sharp, tight suit. My shape bulges under it, the knot bigger than ever, the fabric taut enough to choke. The next suit and the suit after do the same, arrows pointing to the worst parts of me.

I put my old clothes back on. I leave everything in the dressing room. I walk home slow, hands empty.

I TAKE THE TRAIN HOME FOR THE HOLI- day. The whole ride is a blur of landscape and the creep of my old self back into my body.

MY FATHER COLLECTS ME FROM THE station.

I climb into the truck and sit next to him, my favorite feeling. His hair is shot through with silver now. His face has begun its collapse.

"Is that my old dad?" I joke.

"Well if it isn't my favorite daughter!"

"Your only daughter!"

We laugh, the cold winter sun streaming through the windshield. Suddenly, my heart opens a small mouth and whispers: *He's going to die one day.*

The sentence is an arrow through the lungs.

"What's wrong with you over there?" my father asks, bringing his elbow to my ribs, jostling me. "Are you having an asthma attack?"

I picture myself standing over his coffin, his face in repose, eyes closed, makeup covering his dead color, the scent of the funeral home in my lungs, the cheap white satin surrounding him, my beautiful dead father, my shattered heart lowered into the ground, covered in dirt.

- In most cultures of the world, the beginning of family history is set in creation myths
- In his book *Centuries of Childhood*, Philippe Ariès argues that childhood was not understood as a separate stage of life until the 15th century — and that childhood is a recent idea created by nuclear families
- Many sociologists believe the nuclear family fostered the development of industrialization

MY MOTHER LOOKS AT ME OVER THE kitchen table, exhaling smoke.

"It's been so long since I've seen you," she says.

Her arm stretches across the table to clutch mine. Her hand is heavy with rings, so many dazzling rings, then the dark pearls that are her eyes. Her skin sags at the cheeks and jowls, paper-thin beneath the eyes, blue veins showing through the skin.

"I've missed you," I say. I have rehearsed my lines.

"We should see each other more often."

"We should," I agree. "How are you feeling?"

"Well, you know how it is with the knot. But I'm fine."

She stretches her lips over her teeth. The pain is something she hides from me, I can feel it: I imagine her at night, twisted up on her own bed, writhing as I writhe.

"It's been so long since I've seen my mother, too," she says.

By mother, she means the cross with the name etched into it over the grass which holds her mother's body.

She will die too, and then what? My own grief will rise up and riot, I will walk out into the street and scream with a terror that rips my ribs from my body and lifts them up to the sky.

IN THE NIGHT, THERE IS A KNOCK ON MY door.

"Come in," I whisper.

The door opens slowly. My father steps in and makes his way to my bed.

"Want to go on an adventure? Like old times?" he asks.

I can smell sharpness on his breath again, but I nod.

"Nothing crazy," I say.

"Deal," he says. "That's what I was thinking too."

Out in the fields, we walk under the cold moon light. The colors of the world are inverse: Black grass, black sky, white stars, blue light on our bodies. I know the path we are taking. My muscles know the way.

"So, how's the big city treating you? You too good for life back here on The Acres now?"

"You know it's not that. Just hard to get all the way back here."

"What's the job like?"

"A job."

"I knew you'd get one like that."

"You didn't know shit!"

My father lets out a low howl of laughter under the moon.

"I never knew shit, that's true."

"How's business?"

"Not exactly booming," he says.

"What's happening?"

"Well, you know, freight costs are up, demand is down."

"How bad is it?"

"I'd say pretty bad. Some of the harvests have been poor too. The meat coming out of the quarry is just weaker than it's been."

We fall into a silence until we arrive at the gates.

MY FATHER PULLS THE KEY FROM THE thin cord around his neck and unlocks the Meat Quarry. He pulls two flashlights from the pile and hands one to me. The meat scent is thinner than I remember it.

"We've got some new veins here," he says. "Had to find some new paths when the big one dried up."

We wander through the old caverns to the new. The old caverns have meat with less wetness to it, a slight matte to the flesh. Deeper in, the walls get wet again, that new-meat smell thicker, intoxicating.

THE DEEP RED SMELL BRINGS IT BACK: MY body pressed into the walls, into the ground, the taste of his salty mouth on mine, the feeling of him inside of me, my head shaking against the wetness.

My breath leaves my body, I cannot fill my lungs, I stretch a hand out to rest it against the quarry wall, that red moisture beneath my palms again, tears streaming down my face.

"Let's go see this new cavern your brother discovered. Might be some real prime meat there. Come on, get a move on there."

My father shines his light forward and keeps walking. He doesn't notice the dampness of my face, the heave of my back wrenching against the sorrow.

THE NEXT EVENING, THE HOUSE IS PRIS- tine, candles lit across table, my mother in the kitchen, cooking, her knot covered in a red apron. She is her best self. She hugs me close, our knots touching beneath the fabrics.

"There you are," my brother says as he walks in. "What's been going on? Haven't seen you in ages."

I press my head into his shoulder.

"How's quarry life treating you?"

"Good, good, you know — meat and blood!"

"I made your favorite!" my mother chirps. "The red potatoes you like!"

At the table, everything looks cut from a magazine: Red tablecloth, food heaped on plates, full glasses of wine.

"Here's to this family!" my father calls, the sweet sour back on his breath, a glass of liquor in his hands.

"To family!" my mother calls back. We clink our glasses, fill our plates, begin to eat. All of the food is beautiful but cold.

"I never know when to take it out of the oven," my mother says.

They're all going to die one day, my heart calls again.

I PICTURE IT: THREE TOMBSTONES, THREE times my head over the casket, three perfectly still faces in repose, three times the hollow sound of soil hitting casket.

"What's wrong?" my mother asks.

I can't speak, my chest is paralyzed, my lungs won't make air.

"I know you hate coming home," she says. "I know you can't stand it."

My mouth is stuck open, pained, the terrifying future stuck in my head, chiseled into the gray matter of my brain.

"It isn't that," I say finally.

"Just admit that you hate us and you don't want to be here," she says, slamming down her fork.

My throat is so full of love and sorrow that no more words come out. I can't breathe and I know nothing, looking into the heart of the future, the relentless oncoming of death.

"MY BACK IS FUCKED," MY FATHER SAYS that night after dinner. "They've got me whacked out on these new pills."

"Stop digging in the quarry," I say.

"Whose gonna pay for my home when I need it?"

He sits at the table, face contorted, eating vanilla-bean-flecked ice cream.

For a moment, he is the emperor, milk and sugar dissolving against the heat of his mouth.

My mother reigns quietly in the corner, eating nothing, her thin wrinkled hands on the table, two small dead birds.

I VISIT SOPHIA BEFORE I GO BACK TO THE city. She is in a new house. There is her man and her children everywhere. I eat dinner quietly, let the scene absorb me.

"Nice to finally meet you," Sophia's man says.

"You too, I've heard so much about you."

We make painful small talk through dinner: Work, men, the city, the kids, Sophia's new hair.

"So how are you?" she asks after dinner. "How's your exciting life in the city?"

"Oh, it's wild," I say. "I'm out every night. Things are just so busy. Work is great, but the nightlife is something else entirely."

On the train ride home, I sob against the window through which the landscape flashes, back into the city.

I MOVE MY BODY TO THE OFFICE UNDER the black fog of deaths that haven't happened yet. The calendar says Monday.

"What's off with you?" the boss asks.

"Nothing," I say.

"Your eyes are all glassy. You're radiating a bad vibe."

"I'm fine. Just a bit tired."

"Well, don't bring that in here," he says. "Sleep is for the home!"

Outside, the city glints in the morning sun. The knot is a gnarled black pit beneath my blouse, a ticking bomb.

TODAY, IT IS RAINING. I WEAR A THIN dress, no coat, a fool.

The city continues to burst with tragedies:

Three pigeons peck at a pile of vomit.

A woman urinates on the sidewalk.

A man is lifted onto a stretcher, his bony feet protruding from the bottom of the thin sheet that covers his body.

On one corner, a man holds a sign that says: *I have been to war and back!*

The rain pelts my skin through the thin cloth. I put my wet head down.

VISION

I take Jarred out into the throat fields because I need something to strangle.

"It'll be five dollars per," a man in overalls calls to us and I pay.

"It's been a long week at work," I explain.

"I don't understand," Jarred says.

Discomfort blares off his skin in the sun. This is his first time, and I want it to be tender.

In the field around us, bare necks reach toward the sun, short stalks of flesh, the raw edges of the throats blooming the color of old blood at the center.

How did he see me before this? Poised with the right hair. Now, I am disheveled, wearing filthy sweats, bags under eyes.

Lately, the fury has been keeping me up. My anger boils under my skin at work, beneath the fluorescent lights of the office. All I have ever wanted is a soft place. At night, I dream of rooms filled with feathers or cotton which will keep us both safe.

"You don't feel the same anymore, do you?" I ask out in the throat fields.

I can feel his ebbs and flows instantly. I know when he is turning from me in the slightest way, as if the face of a flower toward a second sun, or a planet drifting from its stationary orbit.

"Remember the good days?" I ask. "You loved me once."

He looks carved as stone: No words, just that straight face.

"Say something," I say. The necks keep their stance.

The silence is bigger than suns, it is the silence of distant galaxies. The universe begins to crumble. The rage roars truck-like through my blood.

I throw myself to my knees in the field. I grab a good neck, a thick neck. I look up at him with my mania. The rage multiplies and I wrap fingers around the flesh.

"SAY SOMETHING," I scream.

I clench hard, good around the throat. I squeeze until my fingers want to break. The skin caves in beneath, which feels good, a nasty satisfaction. I strangle harder, until I go dizzy from lack of oxygen, until my rage deflates.

I pant on the ground before him, my weakening fingers loosening around the skin. He stands in the field, still silent. I stare up at his throat which is long and thick, glinting in the light like a golden coin.

This is how love begins to end.

THE GROCERY STORE FLUORESCENTS around me. The packaging of each food is brighter than the last: light green bags wound around bread, bright blue plastic shrouding cookies, vibrant red plastic trapping the body of a cake.

I fill my cart slowly: Meat, eggs, spinach. In the dairy section, the lights get more dazzling, disorienting me.

I'm grasping the handle of a gallon of milk when it happens: The knot seizes, tightens, and pain tears through my body. It radiates out through my limbs, a hell fire in the veins, an eruption that levels me, my mind going blank from the ache.

I COME TO ON THE GROUND. I PART MY eyes, and everything is cool and wet. My knot still hurts, a leftover shiver from the explosion.

"You OK?" asks a man.

I hear him before I see him, before he slides his head into my line of sight. The lights of the grocery store make a saint of his face.

"OK?" I ask.

"Well, you dropped like a shitload of meat all over," he says. "And now you got milk everywhere."

I lift my throbbing head off of the ground and I can feel it — the milk is in my hair, on the back of my neck, on my hands and wrists, a drenching.

"Here, let me help."

He grasps my hand and hauls me up. My body is trembling, wet as if I have just been birthed, milky calf.

"That's it, there you are, just fine," he says. "Do you want me to call a doctor?"

Here comes the sugar water, here comes the sugar water.

"No," I say. "I'm fine."

A grocery store employee walks by and his eyes widen.

"Whoa, whoa, whoa," he says, pulling a walkie-talkie from his green vest. "Clean up in the dairy aisle, I repeat, clean up in the dairy aisle."

I WALK HOME SLOWLY, WITH MY THREE groceries. I can't carry more than that. My knot still aches. Home, I unlock the door, crawl into bed, dried milk on my skin, clothes, in my hair, flaking down onto my sheets like snow.

THE NEXT MORNING, I PICK UP THE DAY'S newspaper from the stand on the way to work. The cover story:

82 DEAD IN BOMB STRIKE

At 7:32PM local time today, our Forces conducted a strike against a foreign country determined to do our country harm. As part of an ongoing effort to contain these attacks against our freedoms, our country dropped a GSU-78 bomb from an aircraft.

We took every precaution to avoid civilian casualties with this strike. There are 82 confirmed dead at the time of press.

I can see them: the 82 dead bodies, their limbs against the ground, their insides splitting open. Their bodies are diagramed in my head: Liver, spleen, intestines, skull fragment, brain, heart.

There is a diagram of the bomb in the paper, and each part of the bomb's body is labelled: Tale plate, base plate, end plate, explosive cavity, suspension lug.

The words *explosive cavity* echo in my head.

The whole walk to work, a chorus of the phrase *explosive cavity* repeats in my head.

"YOU SEE THE NEWS?" ASKS THE BOSS.

"Yes," I say.

"We bombed the shit out of those fuckers, we sure did!" he crows.

"Yes… yes, I guess we did."

"You look sick."

"Ah, just not feeling well today. Still working hard though!"

"Well, let's get back to it!"

At my desk, I stare down into my coffee mug. There is a hard crack in my chest, near my heart, near the breastbone.

IN THE DIM LIGHT OF THE BAR, I SIP THE sharp liquid like my father.

"Long day today?" asks the bartender.

"Very long, how about you?"

"Just getting started! Crazy about this bomb, huh?"

"I hate the bomb. It's terrible what we've done to those people."

"Well, get them before they get us, right?"

A silence begins between us and it doesn't end.

- The word *bomb* comes from the Latin *bombus*, which comes from the Greek βόμβος, meaning "booming," "buzzing"
- Explosive bombs were used in China in 1221, and bamboo-based bombs were used as early as the 11th century
- The Ming Dynasty built fragmentation bombs using iron pellets and pieces of broken porcelain, which served as shrapnel upon explosion
- The Grand Slam is an earthquake bomb that is the most powerful non-atomic bomb used in combat; when it hits, it penetrates deep underground before detonating in order to destroy the foundation of its target

AFTER THE SILENCE, I MEET A MAN WITH blond hair, blue eyes, steel cheeks. He feels silver, cool, metal to the touch. I let his fingers wrap around my leg. I let my hand curl around the back of his neck as if he is mine.

Everything in the world seems to speed up once you learn how it works. Once I caress his neck, there is a quick cut to the apartment.

WE STAND IN THE DIM LIGHT OF MY kitchen.

"Want to hear a joke?" he asks.

"Sure."

"Knock knock," he says.

Before I can respond, a laugh escapes my throat and then our mouths are together. He presses his body against mine, but I hold the knot away from him, an expert now, keep his hands to my shoulders and upper back.

"Want to go to your room?" he asks.

"Sure, but we're taking it slow, OK?"

"Your rules."

"I'm not ready yet," I say.

"That's OK," he says.

In bed, I keep on a nightgown that billows around me. I curl up, my head on his chest. He presses his lips to my forehead and runs his hand over my hair. I fall asleep there, his arms around my shoulders, like maybe our chests are opening slowly, like maybe our hearts are touching through our chests.

When I wake in the morning, he is gone, the sheets cold.

VISION

The women on the block keep showing up with new men. The girl next door started it. She got a brown-haired man. Three doors down, that girl got a man with red hair.

The men are polite and have sparkling eyes, inoffensive new accessories.

Finally, I pull one of the women aside.

"Where'd all these men come from?" I ask.

Her eyes ricochet back and forth, then stop.

"Man Store," she says, all clipped, like she wants to keep the words in her mouth.

"A store?"

"17th and Arch," she says. "That's all I'm saying."

That night, I go to bed muttering it into my sheets:

Man Store

Man Store

Man Store

Like it is a song or a hex. I picture the store, full of men, all of their hearts beating in time.

I save up. After weeks of small meals, I have enough. I move my body out of bed and into the shower, blast off the sleep grime. I dress and put on my face.

The sign says Man Store in black script. A bell sounds when I push the door open.

Inside, thick red drapes cover the walls, jewelry box style, as if someone could lift the roof off and I would begin to spin slowly to a song, that strange tinkling lullaby we all know.

A woman appears before me, wearing a black dress. She has brown hair, hazel eyes, sharp cheeks.

"Can I help you?"

"I'm here for a man, I guess," I stammer.

"Ah," she says. "Have you purchased from us in the past?"

"No. First time."

"Excellent! We do love new clients. What brings you here?"

A torrent of images fills my brain: My cold body sleeping alone, similar to death, my aimless hours. I want to sob when I think about the loneliness of my life, my days like unvisited graves. My eyes fill.

"It's OK," she says. "Let's get started."

I follow her through a slit in the red curtain. We enter a large white room with two chairs in the center.

"Have a seat."

Then the white door opens and it begins.

A procession of men walks in perfect formation through the door, twenty of them, all wearing black shorts, nothing else. They move into perfect lines and rows, their bare chests moving slightly with breath.

"Let's look," she says. "Don't be shy."

The men stare forward, their eyes not even flickering or quivering, strange soldiers.

We move through the forest of them. I smell their skins, soaps, underarms, the difference of their chemistries.

"We have such a large variety that every girl can find something to suit her needs," she says.

I stop in front of a tall man with black hair and olive skin. His jaw is perfect. I can already feel the razor scratch of his stubble on my shoulder. It is already our Sunday morning. My body generates its wants, my soft parts lighting.

I stare into his eyes for a moment and the corners of his mouth twitch to fight a smile. My heart tweaks a bit.

"I like him," I say.

"Excellent choice," she says. "You seem well-suited to each other."

I nod and see him start to nod and stop himself.

"Dismissed," she says. "With #8 on hold for our friend here."

The men file out of the room in an orderly way, including my #8.

"Please," she says, and gestures back to the chair. We sit, my body newly electric.

"You've made a great choice today," she begins. "But we must discuss payment."

"I'm prepared," I say.

"The cost for #8 is $15,000," she says.

"I have $7,000," I say quietly, my stomach shooting through with the thought of never seeing or owning #8, my body hurting with total and absolute want, a lust I haven't felt before.

"That's much too little, I'm afraid," she says. "But there is another option."

"There is?"

"Yes. For the money you have available, you can purchase one half of your #8."

The thought drives a dagger through me.

"By one half," she continues, "I mean that you will select the top or bottom half of #8 and we will perform a simple operation. It's a patented surgery to separate your half. You can take your half home today, or have it delivered."

Sickness rallies inside of me. I can't stand the thought of hurting him. But when I think about leaving him here, everything about the situation goes crystalline.

"Top half," I say, thinking of his twitching corners, of the scruff, of my shoulders.

"Wise choice," she says. "You must care for him."

"Can I come back for the rest?" I ask, heart pounding.

"Yes, as long as no one else purchases his bottom half," she says.

I consider another month of weak meals.

"Yes," I say.

Hours later, she brings him into the red room, where I have been calculating ways to make sure my life accommodates him.

He is perched on a wheelchair, the half of him, the torso up.

"Hello," I say.

He looks up at me with drugged eyes, but the corners of his mouth lift a bit.

"Hello," he says and takes my hand for a moment, which is a beautiful thing, the warmth of our skins. I thank her and steer him away.

I help him into the front seat. As we drive home, he holds my hand over the gear shift and my eyes go wet again, even though we are silent, even though we haven't said a thing.

That night, we lie in bed. He faces me, stares deep into my eyes, and we breathe in rhythm on my sheets.

He takes my face in his hands.

"Thank you," he says. "Thank you for taking me."

He presses his torso against my body and our ribcages touch, the heat of our skins greeting.

Our mouths finally meet and it's a stunner, that kiss, it's like a fireworks finale or a big celebration or a parade and we move our bodies even closer together and our tongues meet and his hands are on my skin and it's so beautiful that I stop thinking about lower halves and checks, and I kiss him back deeply, my man, and I move even closer and I hold the half of him. I hold what's mine.

IN THE MORNING, THE SUN IS STUCK behind gray clouds, a hazy quiet to the rhythm of the world.

I make my way to work. Bleary eyed, I stop for coffee in the shop on the corner. Inside, the walls are done in a dark wood and deep green paint. The coffee seller is cheerful.

"Well, good morning there! What can we get you started today?"

"Just a large black coffee," I say.

"Two coins please."

I slide them across the counter.

"Thank you and you have a great day now, you hear?"

I pour cream into the coffee, two sugars, stir it until it is the right sweet. I lift it to my lips to take a sip and the knot contracts, seizes, cripples my limbs.

I WAKE ON THE FLOOR, THE FACE OF THE concerned coffee seller sliding into my view, the ceiling light creating a dizzying halo behind her head.

"Oh my god, are you OK? Are you OK? Do you want me to call someone?"

I shake my head and slowly wrench my body up from the floor.

The coffee is all over me, my black dress soaked, my head throbbing.

I make it through work, then take my body home, collapse into the sheets, sleep deep.

THE NEXT DAY, MY HEAD IS SORE, POUND-ing. Instead of work, I go to the doctor.

"What seems to be the problem?"

The doctor has black hair, brown eyes, a small mouth.

"Well, I've been falling."

"Falling?"

"My knot starts aching and then I black out wherever I am."

"Knot? What knot?"

"I have a… well, I'll just show you." I stand up and lift my dress. The knot of my torso sits before us in the strange light of his office.

"Well, wow, OK, yes, I see, OK."

"OK?"

"Well, this… this isn't something I see every day, but I have read about it. You and your mother and your mother's mother?"

"Yes."

"I saw your baby pictures in the journals. You know, there has been progress with this."

"Progress?"

"Well, it's not anything established yet, but there's a doctor here who can remove it. The knot."

He slides a thick business card across the table. The card stock is cream colored, thick, perfect. It reads in graphite black:

Dr. Kuznit, Expert Surgeon

"CAN I SEE YOU IN MY OFFICE FOR A minute?" the boss asks.

Outside, the rain has started again. It feels like I have not seen the sun in weeks. The clouds hang low, between the buildings, we walk through them to get to work, fog in the face, the mouth, down the throat.

"Sure."

My heart kicks up an old fear: I'm in trouble, he has caught me doing something bad.

We sit down and stare at each other. For a moment, there's a silence and the amount of trouble I might be in expands to fill that silence.

"Did you ever notice that you're radiating a deep sadness lately?" the boss asks. "And missing a lot of days?"

"No, I haven't noticed a sadness."

"I'd like you to work on it. We agreed you would be a smiling presence here and I just… I don't feel it these days."

The fluorescent lights could be knives, if I reached up. I could shatter one in each hand and go for his throat.

"We have some paperwork here that we'd like you to sign," he explains. "It just says we need you to really work on your sadness. We're willing to help with training."

The paperwork has a sharp edge which cuts my finger. I leave a drop of smeared blood next to my signature, the low slope of my handwriting an acknowledgement.

VISION

The sign on the door says SADNESS TRAINING on a piece of copy paper in thick black letters.

"You must be Cassie," says a woman with short spikey hair dyed blond.

"That's me," I say.

"Well, it's been brought to our attention that you've been bringing your sadness to work."

I nod as if guilty.

"We're going to offer you some strategies to prevent that."

I nod again.

"There are three strategies," she continues. She slides a piece of paper across the desk.

"Strategy number one requires you to put the sadness in another part of yourself. This is called compartmentalization. Think of your sadness and think of stuffing it into a square white box."

I picture my sadness bursting out of a white box in a green field.

"Strategy number two relies on your imagination. You just have to imagine you aren't sad."

I picture myself without my sadness. I picture my sadness in a grave, being buried.

"Strategy number three relies on strength," she says. "I want you to picture yourself digging a grave for your sadness and burying it."

My sadness has a body just like mine. We are the same shape and size. I dig and I dig and I dig until there is a hole big enough for my sadness. I shove the body into the ditch and cover it with dirt.

THE NEXT MAN FROM THE DIM BAR IS A bronze medal: He is not deeply handsome or smart, but here he is.

"I just don't think the government is telling us the full story, you know?" he says, exhaling a cloud of smoke into my face. His voice is high-pitched, his beard admirable.

IN THE DIM LIGHT OF MY APARTMENT, HE is still smoking.

"I don't really smoke in here," I say.

"I do!" he says, smoking.

He stubs the cigarette out and presses his mouth against mine. I become the plume. We move our bodies toward the bed, his hands already on my breasts.

"You're the full meal," he whispers.

I picture it like that: My body a cooked carcass, a side, a dessert, a table set to serve. He runs his hands over the knot, and he doesn't hesitate about it, not even once.

He rests his hands on my hips below the knot before he enters me and our bodies work together frantically.

His hand finds my throat. He squeezes until the lack of air brings stars to the corners of my eyes, until pleasure shakes us.

VISION

The dark loneliness which has been hibernating in my ribs becomes a thick onyx slab that presses down over me.

It takes all of my strength to reach beyond the weight of the slab to pick up the phone. I manage to do it, then I dial the number.

"Thanks for calling Stranger Sleep. How can we help you?"

"I'd like to request a visit."

"Would you like the same as your last order?"

"Yes, please."

"Fifty dollars will be charged to your account. He should be there in ten minutes."

I lean back against the pillow and the next nine minutes stretch black desert miserable, but I face it, I face it head on, I lie beneath the black rock and let it hurt, let it crush the ribs a bit.

When the doorbell rings, I struggle out from under it. I open the door, and he steps into the yellow foyer. He is tall and handsome. I avoid his eyes. Now the loneliness is a large black cube resting in my stomach: square, blunt.

"Hi there," he says.

"Hello."

I move down the hallway and he follows.

It is strange to see him in my bedroom, a rare creature in a new environment. I imagine a bull in a grocery store.

I climb into my bed and he follows suit, then turns to face me. He holds the side of my face for a moment, staring into my eyes. It is a calm look, the bottom of a swimming pool, the loneliness a dark triangle in the center of my chest.

"Now?" he asks.

"Yes, please," and then I roll over, curling, waiting for him to do it.

He moves his body around mine and presses, wraps his arms and one leg around me, buries his face into the back of my neck.

I exhale and go another type of soft, a softness unrecorded before, I sink back into him, rest my body on his thighs, chest, more. He holds tighter, tighter, and then the loneliness gets small, smaller, smallest until it is a pinprick, an inverse star, a dust.

EACH DAY, I MOVE MORE TENDERLY through the city. The pain hides in alleyways, in the shadows, the black sludge of the gut.

I sleep on the floor now, afraid of the softness of the mattress, feathers as a trigger. I never know when I will erupt, a woman as a volcano. A small madness creeps in, a bit of air in the skull.

At work, I stand at my desk, afraid to sit, afraid I will rupture, split.

"Hello, tall lady!" booms the boss. "Is this a power move? Never let the enemy see you at rest!"

I keep typing. The pain from the knot travels up my spine to my brain and floods my wires.

When the pain comes, I leave my body, corpse up like a dead fly on the windowsill, the world hurling itself forward without me.

"I'LL PUT YOUR NAME DOWN," SAYS THE next receptionist. "He can see you in one month."

Her voice sounds like pink syrup, glistening, round at the edges.

"A month?"

"Mhmm! He's all booked up!"

"I'll take that appointment," I say, cradle the phone.

Thirty white squares of hell stretch out before me.

IN THE WILD, I WOULD BE LEFT FOR DEAD
beneath black branches. At sunset, predators would smell my weakness on the air, flesh soaked with sweat, muscles flooded in panic.

I wouldn't fight; I'd lie in the long grass, motionless, memorizing the shape of their teeth in my flesh, knowing them by their mouths as they gnawed through my flesh to my bones.

Fox

Wolf

Bear

Man

I would sing the list in the purple twilight through the black branches of the trees, a sweet death hum.

Fox

Wolf

Bear

Man

VISION

All night the pulsing of the fox hearts in the woods keep us awake. The chorus of the pounding hits the level of dull helicopters.

"What if the walls start to shake?" I ask.

"Don't be dramatic," he says.

It was the same way during the owl season, when their wings stirred up the curtains every night. He never woke then.

The foxes are different. A panic seizes my body at their sounds. The drumbeat continues. I can feel their eyes on the house. I can sense they want us.

All night, their scents work through the windows. Everything smells of their musk, even our towels and bedding.

"We're on the brink of something huge," I say each morning over cereal, which now tastes of their furs.

He is always buttoning his shirt. He slaps my bare bottom whenever I am close enough.

"Don't you remember their heartbeats last night?" I ask.

He shakes his head and puts on a record.

The song spins up into the air. We dance for a moment, our bodies close, the heat between us returning.

We can't know that by nightfall, the foxes will be upon us with their rapid hearts and their gnashing teeth. We won't know how they got in, only that their bodies rush in to fill our living room, a rabid energy to their entrance, the scent of their musks even stronger.

We'll wake with their teeth marks in our skin, not recalling the attack. We won't remember a thing, not even the sweet rare pressure of their wild paws on our skin.

BY THE 30TH DAY, THE PAIN IS SO GREAT I can barely walk.

I take a cab to the doctor's office, collapsed against the busted leather of the back seat, my body grinding against itself.

"Nice day out today," the cab driver calls.

"Yes," I force out. Each letter is a grimace.

I can't notice the sun or the blue sky. I can only writhe. Each pothole shakes the cab and levels a new wave of hell against me.

"Ten coins," he says.

I count them out slowly in my palm, then crawl from the back seat.

The black doors slide open softly. The office is electric white trimmed with dull gray, the colors meant to soften pain. A set of eyes peer over the counter. This time, the eyes are brown, kind.

"You must be Cassie," the eyes say.

"Yes, hello, that's me."

"Well, hi there!" she says, standing up to slide a stack of paperwork on a clipboard to me.

I stare down at the body chart again. I circle the torso twice. This time, I write the number 10 next to the field marked PAIN LEVEL.

"Poor thing," she tuts when I bring the chart back.

I can feel her eyes on my knot. The pain keeps screaming in the background, it reduces everything around me.

"He'll be right with you."

There are no magazines. Instead, a large television on mute displays a newscaster silently moving her mouth. The red banner beneath her face spells out ANOTHER BOMB DROPPED, 150 DEAD in white text, scrolling over and over again, infinite.

Occasionally, the screen cuts to a plume of smoke swallowing land. They do not show the bodies, which must be buried just beneath the cloud.

"Cassie," she calls. "We're ready for you."

I follow her down the bright hallway, white as perfect teeth, pristine. Here, there are no plastic organs, just the glow.

She passes me a gray gown.

"Why don't you put this on and the doctor will be right in to see you."

The gown is soft and warm, but my pain eclipses that. I climb onto the table and curl into a ball.

There is a knock at the door.

"Come in," I call.

Doctor Kuznit appears: Large, olive skinned, dark hair, green eyes.

"Hello," he says, extending a hand.

I slide a hand out to slowly shake his.

"Yes, hello," I say.

"You don't look like you're doing well today."

"The pain is bad."

"Well, let's get you examined. I'll be gentle. Lie straight on the table for me."

I unwind my body and flatten myself on the table.

"Would you mind pulling up your gown?" he asks.

He rubs his hands together to warm them. I pull the gown up below my breasts like always.

"Is it OK if I touch you?" he asks.

I nod. I am ready to be touched by now. I know they will always touch me.

His hands move gently over me. He works his way from the bottom of the knot to the top, stopping to ask: "Does it hurt here? How about here?"

I nod if it hurts there, I shake my head if it doesn't.

"All right now, let's have you sit up so we can talk. Now, it says here your pain is at a 10. Tell me about that."

"It started a few months ago and it keeps getting worse. Sometimes it's so bad I black out."

"Black out?"

"Yeah, like at the store, I don't know — the pain gets sharp and I collapse."

"I see."

He stares deeply at me for a moment.

"That's what we call breakthrough pain," he says. "These are flare-ups of intense pain that are hard for the brain to handle. Your body gets overwhelmed and can shut down."

I nod.

"I'm going to need to run a scan on you, but I think you are a candidate for emergency surgery."

"What, more injections? Is this the sugar water again?"

"No, a surgery. I'm going to remove your knot. It's gotten too tight, and I believe it is choking your vital organs."

"How?"

"Well, first I'm going to make small incisions in the knot to remove the organs."

I imagine him sliding my organs from my body.

"And then I'll remove the knot itself and rebuild your torso with your organs and animal tissue where needed for regrowth."

"What kind of animals?"

"Most often we use skin from a pig or a donor, someone who is dying and donates their flesh."

The lights twinkle above my head. There's not enough air. The facts suck up all of the oxygen.

"I've done smaller versions of this surgery a number of times," he explains. "Largely for women with uneven torsos. These cases aren't exactly the same, but I will do everything in my power to get you back to normal."

MY BRAIN SHUTS DOWN AND THE REST IS like a movie I watch:

The nurses move my body into the scanning machine, drive a needle into my veins to contrast my body and light my insides up like a city, glowing, what a light.

Then the nurses slide a giant needle into the center of my knot, a painkiller, it spreads through me, a perfect springtime, flowers blooming inside of me to block the pain, sweet relief, the drugs a sun shining all through me, my body suddenly a song.

ON THE WAY HOME, I FEEL LIKE AIR, NO pain. I feel the light of heaven rushing through me. I buy a single slice of cake, pure white icing, and take it home with me, the sensation of a parade. I crawl into bed, drug smiling, giant fork, and slide the cake into my mouth, sugar teeth, a laugh escaping my lips.

"SOPHIA," I SINGSONG INTO THE PHONE. "I'm having my knot removed!"

"Wait, what? You sound strange. What are you talking about?"

"I found a doctor, and he can get rid of it!"

"Are you… are you sure that's what you want?"

"Of course it is! Why would I want to stay like this?"

"Sometimes, we just get used to things..." she trails off. "I thought maybe you had gotten used to it."

MY MOTHER ARRIVES TO BE MY CARE- taker.

"What's all this?" she asks, lifting up the papers and pamphlets from the doctor's office.

I must: Fast, eat only ice, strip my fingernails and toenails bare so they can monitor the amount of oxygen in my body.

"Are you sure you want to do this?" she asks.

I don't answer. We both know there is no other choice.

I WAKE UP BEFORE THE SUN RISES. IN THE dark of my bedroom, I prepare for surgery like a strange bride.

I soap myself carefully in the shower. I wash my hair deeply, down into the scalp. I shave my body with the sharp razor.

I towel my body off and dry my hair. I put on my simplest clothes: black cloth pants, black t-shirt, black sweater. I wear no makeup, no jewelry, stripped down to just a body. Each nerve in my system knows it faces a knife.

"Are you ready?" my mother asks, bleary eyed.

"Yeah, I guess," I say.

We climb into a cab. The driver is quiet in the early hour. I can smell the morning on his breath from the back seat.

"Are you nervous?" my mother asks. "I'm nervous."

"I just keep wondering where will I go when they put me under," I say. "Where does the person in me go?"

"Don't think like that. It's going to be fine. They do it all the time."

She reaches over and holds my hand. The sun starts to crest over the horizon. My body presses deeper into the seat with each mile we pass, my fear growing the closer we get.

- In the 1500s, the first German physician successfully synthesized ether

- In 1846, a doctor created "The Ether Dome," where patients were first successfully put under ether anesthesia

- General anesthesia may cause amnesia

- A fully anesthetized brain is not unlike the deeply unconscious, low-brain activity seen in coma patients

THE NURSES ARE A QUIET CHORUS IN SEA- foam green scrubs. Once I change into my gown, they guide me to a large hospital bed with metal railings down the side. I climb up.

My mother clutches my hand, tears in her eyes.

"This is going to be fine," she says, like we're in a bad movie. "Everything is going to be fine."

Then the doctor enters. He looks different this time, in in black scrubs and a face mask.

"How are we feeling this morning?" he asks. "I don't know about you, but I'm feeling good!"

He cracks his knuckles, which will soon be inside of me, a brutal intimacy.

"A little nervous," my mother says.

"Well, you put those nerves aside," he says. "We're going to take good care of Cassie today."

He winks at me over the face mask and it takes on a menacing air since I cannot see his smile. Then things begin to move very quickly.

"All right, you're going to feel a small pinch in your arm and then you're going to drift away."

I nod, then there is a pinch and I do drift away. Soon, there is nothing, just a blank space where my mind was, the needle a guillotine, my body almost a corpse.

VISION

I am nude in the Butcher Field. It is a rite of passage. The air is cool, a shiver across the belly, back, bare bottom, breasts. The landscape is vibrant, stark: gray-lavender pre-storm sky, lush green moss beneath my feet.

Faint bells clang in the distance, then a new rhythm: Feet pounding on the earth, dozens of them, the sound of a stampede until new shapes appear on the horizon.

As they move closer, they come into view: A gang of butchers move toward me in a line, their bodies muscled and broad beneath their uniforms of white rubber aprons, black pants, red rubber boots.

The sky darkens and swirls as the butchers close in. My hands cover my private parts. They circle around me, review my body.

"And what do we have here?" one jeers.

"What a delight," another hisses.

The butchers' faces have bulging noses, strong black beards, aging eyes. Organs are reflected in their pupils — the intestines of lambs, the grassy stomachs of goats, the long-dead hearts of bulls.

"What shall we do with this one?" another one asks.

A silence descends on the group. I can smell death on the land now that they are here. They have been in the white rooms where the blood of animals swirls down sterile silver drains.

"I think we should do the classic," says one butcher. "Just the inventory."

"Yep, that's right, Don," another one shouts back. The bells ring again in agreement.

Two butchers step forward and grasp me by the upper arms.

They lift me into the air and lay me on the moss. The scent of dirt fills my nose, my mouth, my bare body pressed into the young earth. The butchers gather around me again, kneeling, knives in hands.

"Don, why don't you do the honors?"

I scour their faces, trying to determine which one is Don. My question is answered when the gray-bearded man near my knees pulls his knife from its sheath.

"My pleasure," he says.

The rest of the butchers hold down my arms and legs. A butcher near my head places an arm over my forehead, forcing me into the earth.

"Please don't do this," I say. "I'll do anything."

"Now, just hold still, little lady," Don says.

He raises his sharp knife into the air and brings it down to my abdomen, sinking the metal into my skin. Another butcher puts his hand over my mouth to bury my scream.

I smell something wilder than my blood on his fingers. Cold air enters the mouth of the wound, and I shake violently.

"Now, just hold her down," Don says, and their arms get tighter on me, stronger. The pain subsides a bit and I go slack against the earth, each breath a shock.

"So, let's get on in here," Don says. "Time to see what we're working with."

One butcher reaches down and holds the mouth of my wound open. Another butcher slides a hand into the slit. A new sensation begins: I can feel the pressure of his hand, the pain tearing through me, the cold air on my organs.

"Stop it," I moan.

"Well, her intestines are in good shape," he says, giving a squeeze that makes me scream. "Don, you want to check out her liver?"

Don slides his hand into me and up, tearing a new pathway through my body. I feel a pinch on my liver and groan.

"Good liver on this one, good to go there," he says.

More hands enter the wound: They explore me like a strange new terrain, their fingers greedy. Each new motion sends another shot of pain through my body. I tremble against the moss, color drained from my skin.

"Well, that's enough," announces one butcher after they're all bloodied to the wrists.

"You've got some nice organs," says Don. "You'll be fine. You pass inspection."

The bells ring again, and the butchers begin their parade, this time away from me, my viscera on their boot bottoms as they retreat into the horizon.

I'm still on the moss, bloodless, waiting for the earth to swallow me.

MY MOTHER IS THE WOUND-TENDER. SHE has become softer since I've moved away, nicer when she's close to me, when she helps me heal.

"Time to clean the gashes," she singsongs.

My abdomen is a nightmare. It hurts to breathe, to sit up, to swallow, to cough. My mother carries medical supplies, and a small cake. She places the lot of it on my nightstand, then lifts the blanket from my body.

"First the bad stuff," she says. "Then the fun! Now undo that robe."

I untie the cheap robe, fingers fat and clumsy. My stomach is a collision of scars, train tracked, black stitches holding the gashes closed, gnarled caterpillars crawling across my body.

The scent of the secretions floats up off of the wound group. My wounds heal at different paces: Some ooze green, some yellow or clear, others just leak blood.

My mother slathers her fingers in white cream from a long tube.

"Let's start from the top!" she says.

It is strange to see her this way, the caretaker, the kind one.

She rubs the cream over my wounds, one by one, the pressure of her fingers excruciating, making me squirm in the bed. Small moans crest out of my mouth, wave-like. Her knot brushes against my arm as she leans over me. I stay silent.

"Now," she says. "How about some cake? It's like a little party in here!"

She pulls out the vanilla cake. She plunges a fork into frosting.

I let her slide the bite between my lips. I'm just a giant mouth, just lips in a bed.

"WE REALLY SHOULD DO SOMETHING about your face today," my mother says.

I have grown into the mattress by now, part bed, part woman, the sheets ingrained in my skin.

"What's wrong with my face?" I ask.

The painkillers make me mean, hot, flashes of fever shot through the body.

"It could just use, I don't know, something more," my mother says.

She pulls a bag from behind her back.

"I just brought a few things…" she says.

I don't have the energy to fight, so I stay where I am, sink deeper into the bed. She smears the flesh color on my face, then the silver over the eyelids.

"Yes, just like that," she murmurs. "Look how nice, we're getting somewhere now."

She traces black liner over my eyelids, blushes my cheeks, then mascara to spider the lashes.

"There, now," she says, flashing a small mirror at me. "Look how much better you look!"

I STARE AT MY STRANGE NEW SELF, EYES dulled by the pills, face painted bright.

"HOW'S MY GIRL DOING?" COMES MY father's voice over the phone.

"I'm holding up," I murmur, alternating between pain and painkiller bliss.

"That's what your mother says."

"How are you? I wish you were here."

"I know, but I've had to stick around here. We had to close up the Meat Quarry."

"What?"

Even under the drugs, the news hurts me.

"I'm sorry, I know you loved that place. Sure as hell, I did too. But it just wasn't making us money anymore."

I picture it closed up, the red walls fading, the meat scent evaporating. I hang up the phone, pulled back into drugged sleep.

DAY 1: MY MOTHER TENDS MY WOUNDS

Day 2: My mother tends my wounds

Day 3: The wounds are tended by my mother

Day 4: I am a wound tended to by a mother

Day 5: A series of my wounds are tended to by my mother

Day 6: My mother is the tender of my wounds

Day 7: A wound is tended to by a mother which is mine

Day 8: In a garden of wounds, my mother is the gardener

Day 9: A constellation of wounds is named by my mother

Day 10: My wounds are a tender mother

Day 11: My mother tends the wounds and I begin to walk again

Day 12: My mother is the wound-tender and I walk up and down the stairs

Day 13: I tend the wounds and walk the stairs

Day 14: I tend the wounds and sleep

Day 15: I tend my own wounds

Day 16: I am the wound-tender

Day 17: The wounds are mouths to which I tend, my small children

Day 18: Wounds are tended by my hand

Day 19: Alone, I tend the wounds

Day 20: I lose track of the days, tending the wounds

Day 21: I fall into a deep trance at the cut of the light through the blinds, casting patterns onto the walls

Day 22: I pluck the stitches from the wounds like feathers from a bird, strange wires pulled from my body

Day 23: I trace the wounds with my fingers, then I touch myself, thinking of the last man from the bar

Day 24: The doctor's office is brighter than ever.

"How are we?" he winks, lifting my dress.

He traces my wounds with his fingers.

"Very nice. You must've had a talented surgeon," he smiles. "Now, let's see you walk."

I walk for him and he nods.

"Now let's get you back to work," he says.

I put my dress back on, no more robes, no more gowns, no more needles in the veins, no more stitches. I walk out into the world knotless.

I CLIMB INTO THE WHITE PORCELAIN TUB slowly, with care. I wash myself the same: soft motions across the scars with the soap, a low lather across the skin, a gentle raising of the hands to the hair to cleanse the scalp. I move so carefully my mind goes blank.

I WEAR A NEW RED DRESS TIGHT AT THE waist. Pain still shoots from my abdomen, but less now. I make my way to the office. In the streets, the sun shines and it is for me. Joy rises up through the earth into my legs and into my body, the world a beauty I am part of, everything fresh, blank, clean. I walk to the main streets, chin up in the crowd, finally part of the throbbing city.

"What are you smiling about, you ugly bitch?" shouts a man on the street.

"WELL THERE SHE IS!" THE BOSS ROARS, standing next to my desk. "Welcome back! How are we feeling?"

I beam a weak smile. The office hasn't changed the way I have changed: The walls are still dull, the cubicle gray around me.

"I'm great," I say. "How have things been around here?"

"Not the same without you!" the boss says. "Now I can't comment on where you've been, for legal reasons, and I also cannot tell you that you look fantastic, for legal reasons."

"OK," I say.

"Let's make this a great first day back!" he says, and I return to the notes.

IN THE LUNCH ROOM, I SPOON GREEN split pea soup into my mouth.

Brenda walks in, a pink barrette holding her awful bangs back.

"Haven't seen you in a while," she says. "Whatcha got there?"

"Soup," I say, gesturing at the soup.

"What kind?" she asks.

"Split pea," I say, gesturing at the soup again.

"You look different," she says.

I shrug, blush, look down into the sea of soup.

"Guess Dr. Richardson really fixed you up," she says, sliding her sandwich between her thin lips.

I picture myself as a lean new animal. I imagine it: Tearing her limbs from her body, lifting her torso up as an offering to the sun.

I SIT IN THE DIM LIGHT OF THE BAR. THE sunlight only comes through when the door opens. The scent of urine radiates from the bathroom.

A man takes a seat next to me.

"What a beautiful day out, huh?" he says.

I nod. I drink red wine from a splotched glass.

"So, what do you do?" he asks.

"I type notes," I say.

"Nice. I'm in sales."

"I don't know much about sales."

"It's complicated, not worth explaining," he says, loosening his tie.

IN THE DIM LIGHT OF MY KITCHEN, HIS mouth tastes of beer and golden coins. I let his hands run over my smooth abdomen, a belly like all of the other bellies in the world, and he presses against me and then we are in my bedroom and he is sliding my dress off, and in the shards of light from the window, he runs his mouth over my breasts.

I do something I have never done before: Clothing shed, I climb on top of him, legs on either side, and let my body into the light, into full view. I move my body against his, the sensation building between my legs, a heat that will expand, explode. But he is suddenly still, not moving, not touching me.

"What the fuck is this?" he asks. "You're all fucked up. What are these fucked up marks?"

"No, I just had a surgery that..."

He pulls away from me, the warmth of his body replaced by cold air, by nothing.

"I'm sorry," he says. "I can't do this."

Then the familiar symphony: The apartment door shutting quietly, the sound of his car door opening, the engine starting, the rubber, the asphalt, the long silence until morning, the world grinding on the same as ever.

SOME DAYS, I SHED MY CLOTHES AND take inventory of my new body in the mirror.

I am still thin at the arms and legs, brown hair softer and smoother. My eyes glint with a bit of suffering. My lips are still too thin, my jaw more uneven, my ears less noticeable.

My abdomen is flat and smooth now, the rebuilt stomach perfect in shape, taut. But it is marbled with red scars, puckered skin, a mosaic of old stitch work railroading across the flattened land of my stomach.

Sometimes, when I look at myself in the mirror, the world warbles around me, a trick of the eye, as if I am in another life. It feels like staring through heat rising off of the asphalt, the mirage of my new knotless body.

ON FRIDAYS, I SLIDE GOLDEN COINS FROM the velvet pouch. I begin to save some coins in my underwear drawer each week. I save for a vague future that I cannot imagine, but which I can feel coming down on me with the pressure of a burgeoning storm.

IN THE BAR, I PICK UP ANOTHER MAN. This one is short, eyes bloodshot, reeking of old cigars. He doesn't hesitate on my body.

"It's all fair play," he says when I take my clothes off.

He moves against me until he finishes. When he sleeps, he snores. I stare up at the ceiling, still wet.

In the morning, he is gone.

I WAIT FOR MY NEW JOY. I TRY TO SENSE my new happiness like meat in the ground: I press my belly against my bed and wait for happiness to run through my veins like thin gold thread.

My body is slack now, knotless.

At times, I feel limp, worn, a frayed old rope. The photographs flash through my mind: My small knotted body swathed in fabric at the hospital, my mother and her mother before her, me in the yellow lace dress with the pearls around my neck.

There is no photograph of my new body yet. There is no one to take the picture.

I WAIT FOR THE WORLD TO CHANGE around me. I search for a hole where a new life could begin. I look for clues on the sidewalk, in the patterns of the clouds, in the trash cans of the neighbors, in a pile of my hair swept from the floor.

I look for signs: Coins on heads up, four-leaf clovers, rabbit feet, a symbol.

I type the notes. Once home, I cook the chicken. I sleep. I save the coins.

Knotless, my life carries on. The days flick by and nothing changes. It is an endless loop of the same movie, the same woman in motion, over and over and over again and is this a life?

THE NEXT NEW MOON, I DO NOT BLEED.

I GAG LOUDLY, VOMIT IN THE BATHROOM, spirals of bile yellowing the water.

Each night, I pray it isn't true. But I know it in my blood which pounds: *Mother, mother, mother.*

Weeks pass, my belly growing bigger and bigger, a shape different than the gone knot.

"I have made a new knot," I whisper to myself, a hand on the small hard bulge of my abdomen. The scars from the surgery spiral around the new shape. It is as if I have warped my own history again.

- During pregnancy, a woman's heart gets longer and wider so her ventricles can pump extra blood for the child
- In order to prepare for birth, the body produces a hormone that softens the ligaments so the baby can pass through the pelvis during labor
- During pregnancy, the uterus will stretch from the size of a pear to that of a watermelon
- Babies cry before they are born

SOON, I PICTURE IT CONSTANTLY: Me with the child, out in the sunshine. The child reverberates in my bone marrow, a new life emerging from the old.

I close my eyes and try to sense her. I try to make the shape of her out: Her torso, her core.

The same scene plays on repeat: The knotted girl bursting through me, splitting me open like my mother and her mother before her.

THE BOSS PEERS DOWN AT MY BELLY.

"You're sure you're not expecting?" he asks. "Just hitting the donuts a little hard maybe?"

I hunch over my belly to make it look smaller.

"Not expecting anything," I say.

I wait until the bathroom is empty before I retch into the toilet.

In the break room, Brenda looks at my green soup.

"Maybe you want to try a diet or something," she says.

"Not a bad idea," I mutter.

I imagine my hands around her throat.

"I know a guy who can sell you a nice juice cleanse."

I imagine my hands clenching.

I WAKE WET. I SHAKE OFF THE DREAM and sit up in a strange new warmth. Beneath the white blanket, my legs are soaked with blood. The mattress is soaked, slick.

Blood rushes out of me when I stand. I jam a pillow between my legs and make my way to the bathroom.

Skin against the white tile, another wave of pain washes over me. The pain tears through me again and again. I writhe on the floor.

When it subsides, I pant on the ground, face on the cool tiles, body still heaving. I climb up the sink, clinging to the porcelain for strength, my child gone.

VISION

It is pregnancy season. I am big in the belly, my body heavy and aching.

My mother stands next to me. This is called tradition.

She helps me pull off my black dress, revealing my stomach.

"You look just like I did when I was pregnant with you," she says.

She runs her hands over my knot, and I look at my belly with her.

"You're going to make us so proud," my mother says.

My belly extends like the moon, the growth of the child creating new purple marks across my skin.

When the contractions come, they come hard. My mother soaks cloths in ice water and holds them to my face.

Inside, the baby keeps moving, keeps forcing itself down, I am at the mercy of fresh pain. My mother holds me tighter as I twist.

My moans keep coming until my mother's hands appear, holding a black strip of fabric, which she slides between my lips, tying it tight around my head.

"When it gets bad, bite down," my mother whispers.

She moves down to my splayed-open legs, finding another angle to help, a place to put her empty hands.

The black cloth holds tight in my mouth and I bang my fists onto the ground, my roaring muffled.

A huge contraction tears through me, the biggest one, a quarry of red slicing open, a path, the pressure of the child's head breaking through my smaller skin, making it wider, splitting my body.

My mother catches the bloody child in clean hands. The first wails begin.

My mother brings the child to my arms. I look for the only thing I wanted, the only thing that would make me happy.

"She's just like us," my mother says, her voice cold.

I could feel that all along, but prayed it was not true. I rip the black cloth from my mouth and wail.

- Greek women believed they would miscarry if they fainted, got scared, or had strong emotions
- The majority of miscarriages are the result of random genetic errors that make normal fetal development impossible
- Roughly 50% of pregnancies ultimately become miscarriages; often, a woman will not even realize she is pregnant before she loses a child
- Miscarriage occurs in all animals that experience pregnancy; in many species of sharks and rays, stress-induced miscarriages often occur at capture

IN A DREAM, I CARRY MY CHILD ACROSS The Acres and to the Meat Quarry. My child is in a small box. I hold a silver shovel.

I walk through the wintered tunnels, the meat less red now, brown instead now, glisten gone. I take the left, though the walls no longer reach out to touch me.

I dig into the ground where they don't harvest, I dig down into the dirt where they'll never go. I dig until I sweat, until I am covered in the red dust, until I am in a small hole deep as I am tall.

I climb out, chest heaving. I pick up the small box of my child. I press my lips against the top. I try to remember a prayer and no prayer comes.

The box looks even smaller at the bottom of the hole. I move the red soil like a machine: bury, bury, bury.

I walk home slowly, covered in the red.

EACH DAY DEATH WAITS FOR ME. SOME days are clear as a river, others, a black serpent waits in the bush, watches me, ready to curl around my body, clench down, take pink air from lungs. I return again and again to the memories, to the barn, the white house, to the Meat Quarry long since closed, gated up.

VISION

My daughter latches to my breast, pink lips, pink nipple, the flow of milk. It is the morning, golden light through the window, a room of white. Her small hand curls around mine, fingers clenching, the crown of her soft head translucent, downed.

Outside, the world goes by, first a car, then a truck, then a train. A small hum begins in my gut and works its way up to my chest, through my throat, past my lips, the light vibration rocking her as she sucks, nourishing until a thin line of blood works its way into the milk, pinking it, until she pushes my breast away, her mouth opening into a dark red void.

PART III

I RETURN TO THE ADS AGAIN. THIS TIME, I look away from the city, away from the sharpness of the skyscrapers, the elbows, the hard corners of the metal dumpsters rotting in the street.

The ads read:

SHACK AVAILABLE

LAND PARCEL EXPIRING, CHEAP

75 ACRE VACANCY WITH ELECTRIC NEAR ROAD LAKE ACCESS ACRE MUST GO

SMALL CABIN FOR RENT

I circle the fourth listing, then go into the country. The train hauls its body over the tracks. The sun glints through the window and my hollow womb echoes back.

Flashes as we cross the landscape: My mother's hands and their specific sunspots, my father's stale scent in the morning, the pattern of my brother's beard patching across his cheeks.

The small town is in the country, but far from The Acres and my parents. I step out of the tiny train station and into the town proper, four blocks of shops: a bar, a grocery store, a post office. Blue-black mountains rise up beyond all of that.

I follow the directions and move through the blocks, then take a few lefts and a right down a dirt road. An old man waits next to a mailbox, his eyes watery and blue.

"You look a little fancy to be all out here," he says, gesturing at my dress. His denim jacket is worn, dust on his boots. He is not new.

"I have other clothes."

"Got a feeling this isn't for you, out here."

"Why?"

"Smaller than the city."

"Just let me take a look."

He gives me a hard squint.

I FOLLOW HIM DOWN THE PATH TO THE small cabin. The cabin is painted red, the color of old blood. Inside, the walls are freshly painted. The cabin offers: A small bedroom, bathroom, cramped living room with wide widows, a kitchen with a small stove and a small silver sink.

Through the windows, I can see a lake glistening in the distance.

"I'll take it," I say.

This sentence is followed by a series of transactions.

BACK IN THE CITY, I LIVE A HALF-GONE life for weeks.

"I'd like to resign," I tell the boss. His face is rutted with wrinkles by now. Where have the years gone?

"Resign? What for? The company needs you."

I picture the company as a child: A series of cubicles with eyes and a mouth which is pressed against my breast, latching.

"I'm moving away."

"You had a strong future," he says. Anger rises in his face.

"My last day will be in two weeks," I say gently.

"Ungrateful, always were," he whispers. "You have betrayed us."

EVENINGS AND WEEKENDS, I FILL THE open mouths of empty brown boxes with my life. Clothing, bedding, small statues and rocks, a single photo of my brother, the remaining soaps and shampoos from the bathroom. The objects of my life take on more weight when combined.

Soon, there is only my mattress on the floor with a lamp beside it. I sleep there unmoored. Each night, I dream of knots: Squares, lariats, double bows, rolling hitches, surgeons.

- The clove hitch is the weakest of all common knots
- To loosen a tight knot, one must rub it against a rock or soak it in water
- The Mystic Knot is a combination of six infinity knots and a symbol of long life full of good fortune
- Whenever a piece of rope is knotted, it is weakened

EVENTUALLY, THERE IS ONLY THE bareness of my apartment, virtually scrubbed of me, more sense of ghost.

ON MY LAST DAY, I SIT IN THE LUNCH-room, spooning green soup into my mouth.

Brenda sits across from me, sliding bland crackers into her mouth.

"We dropped another bomb today," she says through the crumbs.

The sound makes me murderous, rage in my blood.

"You know, they deserve what they get," she says.

I can picture it: Me slamming her body to the ground, then doing something deadly. I wash my soup bowl in the silver sink. I do not say goodbye to Brenda.

IN THE REARVIEW MIRROR OF THE moving truck, the city stays static. I half-expect the skyscrapers to collapse or explode. But the knives stay upright as always, glint once more in the sun, the city grinding on.

I UNPACK MY LIFE INTO NEW arrangements.

I feel sure, during moments of unpacking, that I have moved to this town to die. I have no work to do here, only my savings of gold coins to chip away at.

AT NIGHT, THE QUIET OF THE COUNTRY roars, the sound loud and dark as a void. I can hear my organs grinding against each other beneath my blanket. I can hear my ovaries begin their monthly symphony.

MY DAYS PASS ALONE. I DON'T SEE anyone. I keep my body inside the cabin. I don't brush my teeth. I sleep like a dead woman. In my dreams, I am still knotted. In my dreams, I am knotted and I am digging holes in an endless field. The dirt rises up around me like dirty palaces.

FINALLY, I NEED FOOD. I WALK TO THE grocery store. The sun beats down on the dust, which kicks up around my footsteps. The light inside the grocery store is not fluorescent but a warm yellow.

I fill a small basket with red meat, eggs, spinach, lemons. The cashier has her hair pulled back, no makeup.

"New here?" she asks, as if newness is a disease.

There's a sharp intake of breath behind me, and I turn around.

The man in line brightens into view: He is tall, bald but with a thick dark beard, dark flashing eyes. He wears a blue button-down shirt and dark jeans.

THE STORE SEEMS TO RATTLE AROUND us. Our eyes finally meet. I have the sudden urge to place my hand on the side of his face, tenderness surging in my chest.

"Yes, new," I say to her while staring at him.

"You've got a lot to learn about it here…" she rattles on, but I can now feel the axis of gravity. I can sense the planets rotating in their orbits. Now that I have seen him, I can see the pyramids, all the intense deep secrets of our distant lands and all of the world's history.

I turn and leave.

I HUNCH OVER THE SMALL SILVER GUT OF the sink. I cut the lemons down the center one by one, arms shivering against the knife. Then, I run the yellow halves over the walls until they glisten at a higher voltage, until the house radiates the smell, until it smells as if my mother is beside me.

"HOW'S THE COUNTRY TREATING YOU?" comes my father's voice over the line.

How to say it: The sunrise could cripple your heart, the lake glistens better than the eyes of all men, the moon is larger than all moons combined and stands on the mountains each night to keep watch over my body?

"It's great. I love it here, I really do."

"Well, you know we miss you."

"Tell her we miss her!" comes my mother's voice from the background.

"Do you want me to put your mother on?"

"No, not right now. Next time."

I climb into bed alone, the world vibrating around me, the silence and moonlight. I picture again the flash of his eyes.

ALREADY, LOVE HAS SEIZED ME. A NEW light prisms through my chest. I move through my daily motions drugged, dazed, the world tinged by the sensation: Pink trees, pink grass, pink clouds, pink sky, the sweetness of the world finally shown to me.

- Love can occur in a fifth of a second
- Falling in love produces several euphoria-inducing chemicals, stimulating 12 areas of the brain at the same time
- One symptom of hypopituitarism, a rare disease, is the inability to feel the rapture of love
- Upon looking at a new love, the neural circuits typically associated with social judgment are suppressed

A FEW NIGHTS LATER, I CANNOT SIT STILL. I walk the road through the small town to the small bar. The small bar is built of thin metal, even the door, which I push open.

Inside, two men hunch over their beers. I sit down two stools away and order a drink.

"You're the new city girl, huh?" one of the men asks.

"I guess that's me."

"You won't last long out here."

The other man cackles.

"Last one only made it three months. Might've had your cabin if I recall."

"Sure did," the other one coughs.

In the silence after, I stare into my glass. The sad song my father used to play in the car comes through the jukebox in the corner. A sad feeling floods my heart, and my eyes well up with tears. I blink them back.

The door opens and the man from the grocery store steps in. The air exits my lungs and I cough as he takes the stool to the left of me.

"Rye," he says, and the glass appears. He keeps one hand in his jacket pocket, the other around the rye.

We sit like that for a moment, sipping our drinks, before he turns to me.

"You're the new girl."

"That's what they keep calling me."

"What's your real name?"

"Cassie. Yours?"

"Henry."

"Nice to meet you."

We don't shake hands.

"Where'd you move from?"

"The city."

"You got the red cabin, then?"

"That's me."

"I saw you moving in. Few days ago, right?"

The sentence hangs there. I will treasure it and examine all of its intricacies later: The way his eyes must have been on me and my boxes full of my life.

"What do you do?" I ask.

"Mostly fix every engine in town. What about you?"

"I'm not really sure yet. I just quit my job."

"Must be nice."

"I grew up at The Acres," I blurt out.

"Out by the Meat Quarry?"

"You know it?"

"Of course, that place is a legend around here. I've never seen it. What is it like?"

His eyes peer into mine. It is live wires when he does that, the voltage between us.

"It was beautiful. I used to harvest meat with my father and brother."

He sits back.

"I'm impressed, a young kid doing that."

"I was great at it. Why do you love motors?"

"You're changing the subject."

"I am."

"I'll allow it. I love motors because working on them teaches you to think different ways around a problem. It's personal work, meditative even. The sum of all parts makes them come alive. That's fascinating to me."

I picture my young arms ripping meat from the quarry walls, a small flesh-covered machine.

"I think I understand."

The sentence hangs thick between us — it is bursting with recognition, the light of our minds meeting.

"Did you know we're all engines, because by their most basic definition, engines are machines that convert energy into motion?"

My heart responds with a crescendo, a wave that rises and holds high as we talk long into the night, until we are out in the midnight gravel on the road outside of the bar in the moonlight, until his lips are on mine and a new song begins.

I WAKE IN BED ALONE, IN LOVE, NUDE. I grind my bare body into the soft bedding, the comforter warm on my bare skin. I picture his face and grin up into the morning light.

- An engine is designed to convert one form of energy into mechanical energy
- The first internal combustion engine was built in 1807 and was used to power a boat up a river in France
- Karl Benz is credited with building the first car engine in 1886
- A large engine can have up to 1,400 different parts

VISION

Henry and I take our heads off in order to be intimate.

"Be gentle," I say.

I am nervous, heart racing, eyes fluttering as Henry slides my head from my neck.

I see the world from strange new angles: flashes of the ceiling, then Henry's face, then the lower half of his body.

I look up at our bodies from my new place on the floor. I can feel the wood against the newly raw end of my neck.

A body can control itself without a head and mine does. I slide his head off of his neck and place it next to mine on the floor.

Our two heads stare deep into each other's eyes.

Next to us, our headless bodies sit together with their legs crossed.

Our bodies move toward each other without our heads. I want to touch his hand, but the scene is too intense.

Our bodies are finally close enough. Then our hearts emerge up from our throats. Their round shapes peek out like big red pearls. I feel shot through with arrows.

Ever so slowly, our throats find each other, and our exposed hearts touch.

Light shoots through my limbs and head. The world is a clear morning. All fog dissipates and there we are, Henry and I, standing on a mountain near a stream, eternal.

IN THE AFTERNOON, I READ A BOOK ON the couch. I can barely catch the sentences, I can only imagine Henry's lips, the history of the entire world in a kiss, various genealogies of flowers blooming each time our mouths touched, how first I smelled lilac, then rose, then hyacinth, wet from the garden.

A knock at the door shatters my trance. I open the door to find Henry standing outside, his hands in his pockets. He flashes a grin when he sees me, but there is a slight fracture to it.

"I had to see you," he says.

Then I am in his arms, our mouths together, he is holding me as I have never been held, out in the bright light of day. We move into the house, to the sofa, our bodies pressing together in a furious heat. He finally disentangles himself from my limbs and we sit beside each other.

"I have to tell you something," he says.

He slides his left hand into view. A band of gold glints on the ring finger, and a tear rips through the universe. The planets quit their motion. The seas pause. The clouds hesitate, frozen in the sky. The sun, for a brief moment, does not burn.

"It's not exactly what it looks like. It's very complicated between us right now. There's been no love there for some time now."

"But you kissed me…"

"I wasn't expecting to meet you."

"But what…"

"We don't sleep in the same bed," he blurts.

The sentence hangs there. I stare at the curious shape of it, the strangeness. My heart is a cavern, dug out with the shovel of the fact.

"It's not that I want to stop seeing you," he says. "I just had to tell you the truth."

His eyes voltage into mine again. I picture a wife in the distance: She is older, her face sagging, her body collapsing.

"Do you want me to leave?" he asks.

But then our mouths are together. Everything he's told me is erased by the glow of it, the electric thrill tunneling through me.

He presses me down into the couch, our hands searching each other's bodies, his fingers tugging my dress up. My scars chill in the new air.

His mouth roves down to my stomach, and I catch my breath: Soon he will see the marks on me. He pauses over the lines and looks up. Our eyes meet.

"It doesn't matter to me," he says.

He slides back up and our mouths meet again, then our clothes are gone, our skins pressing, our bodies becoming the same trembling arch.

- He grew up on the coast
- His parents are still married
- He has a garage at the edge of town full of parts of engines. I smell grease on his hands when he comes to me. In the garage, the metal parts gleam even in the dark. I watch him work: Squinting eyes, rapid-fire tooling, the precision with which he moves until it roars to life
- He is an only child
- His favorite color is silver
- He once climbed the world's greatest mountain
- He tells me an octopus has three hearts, nine brains, and blue blood, then he runs his hands over my body

WHAT THEN IS A WIFE? I TWIST THE word over in my head.

I try to find her in town. I check the post office, the grocery store, the small shop which sells both jewelry and pipe supplies. The husband and wife each own half, eye me suspiciously over their metals.

"What are you looking for?"

"Nothing," I say and leave.

I spend nights picturing her: Brunette, then blond, then raven-haired. She has phases like a moon.

STILL, WE PERSIST. WE MEET AT THE small bar or he arrives at my cabin with offerings: Small donuts, wines, fresh cherries by the handful.

It begins the same way each time: My door opens, then I am in his arms, our mouths against each other, unable to speak, only the rushing pink language of our bodies.

I stare up into the wild sky of his face and a new chamber of my heart expands, a fresh gust of wind through the red chambers.

THERE ARE SIMPLE SCENES TO COMPRISE a love: His body against mine, another definition of skin and pleasure. After, head against his chest, his hand dangling over the small of my back, fingers trailing lightly there, a place even the wind rarely touches.

WHEN HE TOUCHES ME, HE NEVER HESI- tates to touch my scars.

- The word *wife* is of Germanic origin, from Proto-Germanic *wībam*, meaning *woman*; unconnected with marriage

- The word *adultery* derives from the French *avoutre*, which evolved from the Latin verb *adulterare*, meaning "to corrupt"

- In parts of the world, adultery may result in honor killings; women who committed adultery were often stoned to death or given 100 lashes

- Men who committed adultery were often imprisoned for one year

- In pre-modern times, it was unusual to marry for love alone

I AM IN BED WITH HENRY IN THE SUN-light. His hand is on my hip. We face each other. I slide my hand onto the side of his face.

We stare into each other's eyes. I have never done this before and it makes my breath catch.

"I am completely infatuated with you," he says.

VISION

I am about to bloom, I can feel it. I have always been seasonal in this way. I wait on the bed. Waves of warmth rush through me, small fevers that build and recede.

"What are you doing in there?" Henry calls from the living room.

"This happens every few months," I say.

I have been keeping track on a calendar.

"What happens?" he calls. "What are you talking about, babe?"

My skin has already begun to green. Another blast of warmth tears through my body.

"It's too late," I say.

I begin to bloom.

Leaves pierce through then grow up out of my skin. Vines bloom then wind their way down to the floor. Ferns and grasses sprout beneath my armpits, between my legs. It hurts but nicely. Near my upper thigh, a single fragrant blossom emerges from a bud, peeling open to reveal deep purple petals.

I power the whole scene. My body is a rainforest conduit, an entire new ecosystem in our bedroom. I flourish like Brazil.

Henry steps into the bedroom and finds me wild, green, lush. His jaw drops.

"What the fuck, Cassie?" he asks.

But I stay silent to let him see me this way. Then he does the right thing. He takes a step closer, then presses his face into the blossom. I hear him inhale, nodding his face against the softness.

I LOVE HIM WITHOUT THOUGHT or regard. The sky has never been so wide or so blue.

THE NEXT DAY, WE STAND BESIDE THE lake.

"There are 117 million lakes on earth, covering roughly 4% of the continental surface," he says while our hands are clasped together and all of the doubt rushes from my mind for a moment, his wife receding into the distance, a motionless mountain, her breasts and belly part of the landscape now, nothing to do with us.

MY JEALOUSY DOES FLARE. IN THE evenings, alone, I hurt myself with a series of harsh scenes:

- Their bodies back together, familiar, gold rings flashing off the nudeness of their moaning pleasure

- An undying confession of her love written into a letter which he is reading, his heart full of joy

- Their bodies next to each other in bed, touching, soft and warm, her face buried into my place of his neck

VISION

The shop says JEALOUSY REMOVAL over the door in fat red fluorescent letters. A bell dings when I step in. The entrance gleams white and silver.

"Hey," comes the drawl from the old man behind the counter.

"Hi," I say.

The old man has white hair, jowls, and blue eyes.

"You here for the regular?"

I nod.

"You sure?"

I nod.

"Your first time?"

I nod.

"It is a permanent procedure and we cannot be held liable for any side effects or other repercussions."

"I understand."

"Well, here's the paperwork. We do it cheap out here. Gonna cost $110, gonna need your ID."

I scrawl out my name and my answers, then fish my license out of my purse, pass it all over.

"If you're ready, I'm ready," the old man says.

The room is white-walled with a white table in the center. There are silver countertops and cabinets. I sit in an open-backed paper gown.

"Now, let's see what we're dealing with here."

He steps closer to the table, and passes a hand under the gown, over the bare skin of my back. He runs his fingers between my shoulder blades until he finds the thick lump on the left.

"It's a big one," he mutters. "Jesus."

He shifts his fingers over the lump again.

"Now, we won't need to knock you out for this, just a topical painkiller," he says. "It's going to hurt a bit, but it'll be worth it in the end."

He gives me two injections near the bulge. Then, he moves a scalpel expertly over the lump. I cry out in pain as the skin splits and air rushes into the new wound.

"Hold still now," he says.

I feel his hands on either side of the fresh wound. He applies pressure and the mouth splits. I can feel the lump sliding out of me.

"There it is," he says.

He brings his hand forward to show me. All of my jealousy has crystallized into a disgusting gem, slick with my blood, shining its evil in the fluorescent light.

He stitches me back up, puts my skin back together.

I put my clothes back on, moving slow, wincing at the pain. I move down the long white hallway to the front counter. He's waiting there, and in his hand is the black gem, clean and shining, sparkling less without the blood.

"It's yours to keep," he says. "We don't want all of your baggage."

"What do I do with this?" I ask.

"Most people toss it in the pit up the street," he says. "Follow the signs."

The signs are small and wooden. They spell out JEALOUSY PIT in sloppy black script with jutting arrows pointing the way.

I park and get out of the car, walking up to the edge of the pit.

Below, a quarry in the earth is full of them, jealousy gems, all black, removed from everyone in town and left here.

I picture the whole town split open like me, their incisions like smiles. I stare down into my stone again, into that dark, awful crystal. Then I throw it down with the rest.

"I'M IN LOVE," I SAY OVER THE PHONE to Sophia.

"In love? What's his deal? Who is this now?"

A baby cries in the background.

"Well, it's complicated. He's still married."

The silence makes the line fizz between us, all the electricity in the wires suddenly roaring.

"Well, this is a disaster," she mutters.

I've already done the shrinking within. The wife is small inside of me now, a chess piece, a queen carved of ivory nestled between my ribs.

VISION

I vomit small islands into the toilet. Then I sit perfectly still as a woman applies my makeup. She is close enough for this to be an intimacy, her proximity to my skin, my bad teeth.

"Big, special day," she murmurs, colors scattered around her — foundations, blushes, eyeliners, mascaras.

She blends the colors onto my face, the face over my face, the new mask.

"How do you feel today? Excited?"

"Yes, of course! Just my nerves..."

I wear a white satin robe and the small sweat of a bride.

"You're so cute," she hums. "Don't worry, love is beautiful. Your whole life! Together!"

My mother appears over her shoulder, eyes painted.

"Are you sure she's using the right colors, Cassie?" she asks. "Are you sure those are the ones you want?"

A photographer snaps a picture.

"Don't take my picture! My face is all wrinkles!" my mother snaps. "Kidding, kidding, but just don't."

The woman moves on to my hair, the heat of the curling iron cutting through the robe, the scent of my burning hair lacing the room.

"Gosh, how beautiful," my mother says. "Are you sure you don't want to put your hair up? I always thought you'd put your hair up!"

My hair curls down around my shoulders. "I'm sure," I say.

"It's gown time," the woman whispers, final touches on my hair done.

"OOOOOOOH!" my mother shrieks as the camera flashes again.

"CAPTURED! So realistic!" the photographer calls.

"Come here," my mother says.

I move closer to my gown, which hangs lifeless on the hanger, sparkling in the sun.

"Now, let's get that robe off," my mother says. "Slowly, slowly."

I shed the robe, standing in my white satin underwear set as she and the woman gently pull down the gown and unzip it slowly.

"Now, in you go," my mother says.

I step into the open foaming mouth of the gown. My mother pulls the bodice up around me and pulls the zipper up just as slowly. She turns me around to face her.

"Oh my god," she says. "Just oh my god." Another camera flash.

"Come here," she whispers, clenching my hand, drawing me to the mirror. The gown is heavy on my body, as if made of coin.

"Are you ready to see?" she asks. "Yes," I say.

She spins me around by the shoulders, her nails pressing into my skin.

"Would you look at my perfect daughter?"

And there I am in the mirror: Perfect, smooth waist trimmed in sequins and tulle, perfect makeup, a face like someone else's face, a magazine face.

"You're a dream," my mother exhales, eyes gleaming.

Henry waits at the end of the aisle, I know. I can feel him there, standing next to my father. I stare into the mirror, at the new costume layered over me, camera flashing again and again, my heart suddenly wild with joy.

I KNOW WHAT LOVE IS NOW, AND HOW love likes to behave.

AT NIGHT, HENRY SNORES BESIDE ME. Occasionally, he stops breathing altogether for long moments. Fear makes me softly prod him in the ribs until he fills his lungs with air again. I go on like this all night, pulling him back from the ledge of death.

- The name Lazarus can be sourced to the Greek *Lazaros*, meaning "God hath helped"
- In the Bible, Lazarus is the name of a man who was resurrected by Jesus in one of his most spectacular miracles
- Lazarus has become a metaphor for rebirth, recovery, and rehabilitation

"LAKES CAN APPEAR OR DISAPPEAR," Henry says. "It all depends on the levels of groundwater or draughts."

Then we are naked again, we are making love again, we are never not touching, we are never not making love.

All the history of the world has led up to this, to the rushes of pleasure between us, to our sweats mingling, to our loud call back to the universe.

VISION

I wear a diamond ring on my left hand. Each evening, we come home from work and sit down to a beautiful dinner of roast chicken, vegetables, and glasses of wine.

After dinner, he reaches across the table to squeeze my wrist. Then, we collapse into bed again, exquisitely touching until morning.

I CANNOT SEE BEYOND HIS LIGHT. I cannot see the cracks in the ground or the wife, until one day while I am running errands alone.

It is a quick glimpse: She stands outside of the grocery store with Henry, not touching. His face seems strained in the sun or else my wishful thinking contorts his features. They step into the store.

She is not at all what I pictured: Black hair, sharp nose, full lips, wide hips.

I absorb the full blow of the scene, which takes a left punch to my jaw, shattering bone. I walk home, weeping in agony. Once home, I howl into my pillow as if a shot animal, bleeding from the gut, the red of life rushing out from the hole.

"A SUBGLACIAL LAKE IS A LAKE THAT IS covered by ice," Henry says.

He touches me then, and the touch is a song which I have heard before and will hear again and again.

NOW WHEN SOPHIA CALLS, HER VOICE strains over the line.

"How's it going with him?"

Our bodies are constantly in bed, our hands always roving, how do I say it is a drug?

"Fine, thank you," I try. "How are the kids?"

"They're driving me fucking crazy!"

Something shatters in the background, then screaming.

WE MAKE LOVE AND IN THE MORNING, WE eat cake for breakfast. His mouth is full of frosting. I taste it later when we kiss goodbye.

ALONE, I STARE OUT OF THE WINDOW AT the lake. I am dazed again. I climb back into my bed, bask in the fading scents of our bodies.

The phone shrills.

"Hello?" I ask.

"Come home," my mother says. "Your father's heart is acting up."

WE SAY GOODBYE AT THE TRAIN STATION. Henry kisses me deeply in the sunlight. My heart isn't in it. My heart is already on the train home, gone.

ON THE TRAIN, THE LAND SHIFTS through the city and the wilderness. I see the skyscrapers then the dead body of a deer in the brush. A man snores next to me.

In my head, I hum *aorta* to calm my nerves.

The train pulls to a stop and I gather my bags. I climb down the silver steps and find my brother waiting for me with the red truck in the parking lot. He hugs me tight.

"Well, if it isn't my long-lost sister," he says, eyes watery and drawn, the joke landing false even as he makes it.

"What's happening with Dad?" I ask.

"He said his heart felt tight this morning. He was having trouble with feeling anything in his arms."

I nod and climb in the truck next to my brother. He navigates us over the land, we stay silent.

The house comes into view. The asphalt beneath my feet feels too soft. My brother pushes the front door open, and my mother is crumpled on the ground, sobbing.

"He's gone," she says between heaves, as if her heart is stopping and then restarting.

"Gone?" my brother shouts. "Gone? Why did you make me go pick her up?"

He collapses next to my mother.

THE WORLD WARPS AROUND ME, THE walls bulging and receding, the ground swelling and pulling back in waves. My head bobs slowly up and down, tears streaming down my face, grief obliterating everything inside of my body. My brother holds my mother as she shakes and sobs.

"Go be with him," she calls. "I don't want him to be alone, he shouldn't be alone! Cassie, go be with him!"

I do not want to see my father, but I move up the stairs slowly in the strange air of the house. I push his bedroom door open, heart pounding so slowly it might be stopping.

DEATH HAS JUST BEEN HERE, I CAN SMELL it. My father's body is in the bed, tucked into the covers. I don't want to move closer, but I move closer. I don't want to see him, but I must see him.

At the bedside, I stare into his face: Eyes open wide, staring at the ceiling, drained of life, face settling back into itself, nose still a large red mountain, his mouth gaping open, rigid, as if stuck in one last slow scream.

I know I should cry, but no tears come now. Instead, I take his hand in my hand, his skin feels wrong, cold, gone, ended.

LATER, MY MOTHER FINDS ME IN THE living room, her eyes bloodshot, hair at strange angles.

She sits down on the couch beside me and then crumples, her knotted body going limp, her head falling into my lap.

"I don't want to live anymore," she says into my legs.

She quivers against me. I rest my hand on her knot. I stare deep into the mouth of a new void.

THE NEXT MORNING, IT HITS ME WHEN I wake. I gasp for breath in my old bed, eyes to the ceiling, my father, my father, my god, my father, gone.

- The word *grief* is derived from the Old French *grever*, meaning "afflict, burden, oppress," and from the Latin *gravare*, meaning "to make heavy"

- Grief is a multifaceted response to loss, particularly to the loss of someone or something that has died, to which a bond or affection was formed

- After conducting two decades of research, researchers determined there were five trajectories to grief:

  Resilience

  Recovery

  Chronic Dysfunction

  Delayed Grief or Trauma

  Suicidal Tendencies

I TRY TO RECALL HOW HENRY FELT, WHAT it meant to kiss him. My mourning is too thick. I remember nothing, even when the phone rings, even when it is his voice through the line.

MY FATHER'S WILL INCLUDES INSTRUC-tions: The Acres will be sold, the profits divided by three among us, and he will be reduced to ash.

VISION

Ten years old, in my father's truck, the wind whipping through the window as he drives us over The Acres. His hands are rough on the steering wheel from hauling meat. He doesn't smell like liquor.

"I don't tell it to you enough," he says. "I'm not really that way, you know."

"Tell me what?" I ask, distracted by the land whipping by.

"I do love you," he says.

"Love you, too."

Then it gets quiet. He keeps driving like nothing has happened, though there is a small warmth in my young chest. His favorite sad song is playing on the radio. Tears begin in my eyes and I hide them by staring out the window.

THE ROOM IS MAGNIFICENT IN SIZE. IT IS cold, refrigerated. My father's body rests in the center, draped in the white sheet.

"I simply need a family member to identify," says the coroner. He has a nose as if from a statue, skin waxy and un-sunned.

My mother wails from the hallway where my brother holds her. It has stayed this way since his death: My brother holding my mother while I make the arrangements.

"Are you ready, miss?" he asks.

I nod.

He lifts the sheet and I see my father again.

His face sits still as a mountain, the high peak of his nose, the valley of his lips. His mouth is no longer frozen open, his eyes too are now lines.

"How did his mouth close? How did his eyes close? Who closed them?"

"Miss?"

"Who closed his mouth? How did it come to close?"

"We took care of that very gently, miss. It is a delicate thing."

A cold body now, stiffer than when I last saw him, clenching in on itself. I reach to touch his hand beneath the sheet, and I draw back from the claw it has become. He is no longer hauling meat, no longer drinking, the breath gone. The ache in my heart could stop the world, stops my own breath so I am like him for a few still moments.

"This is my father," I say.

The coroner drops the sheet.

"That's all, miss," he says.

He guides me away from my father. I can still feel the pressure of his hand on my lower back, propelling the base of my spine.

Then we get into the car and I drive us home, my mother trembling in the front seat. Later, in the night, they start their fires for his body.

- During cremation, the body is placed in an oven that reaches 1,650 degrees Fahrenheit

- Large magnets pick up metal fillings and body replacements after cremation

- A pile of bones is left behind after cremation

- The bones are ground into ashes which are given to the family

BEFORE THE SERVICE, WE CREATE A COL- lage of his living. In snapshots: My father laughing in the quarry, my father young in swim trunks next to the river, my father as a chubby child, my parents on their wedding day, eyes roaring like hot stars.

NIGHTS, MY MOTHER SEIZES WITH HER grief until the prescriptions come in. Then, we gather around each evening to slide the white pills into our mouths, the three of us, our new ritual. I climb into my childhood bed, sleep thinly.

- The custom of wearing unadorned black clothing for mourning dates back to the Roman Empire, when dark-colored wool was worn during mourning

- In the 1300s, the color of deepest mourning among medieval European queens was white

- In Hinduism, death is not seen as a final end; relatives should not weep, but perform funeral rites to the best of their ability

- In Judaism, the central stage of mourning is Shiva, which occurs for the seven days following the funeral; mirrors are covered, and a small tear is made in an item of clothing to show a lack of interest in personal vanity

THE VIEWING IS OF MY FATHER'S URN, which is a large metal sphere. We set up the collages of my father's life around the urn, which gleams its fresh silver in response.

The crowd is thin, a few men from town, a few distant uncles. Sophia arrives with all of her children, who cling to her or climb beneath the chairs and rattle the legs like prison bars. I cannot keep track of them all. She hugs me in close.

"I'm so sorry," she says into the pink curve of my ear.

But I am no longer in my body. I am orbiting the scene, I am a moon floating above the voices reading the eulogy, above my body as I recite the old poem he loved, above the orchids which turn their deep faces toward my father, the man now made of ash.

VISION

We ring the brass bells three times. The noise echoes through all of the streets in the town. The sound is followed by the quiet of mourning. The sound of the bells rung three times means only one thing: The king has died.

The king's body is a bed in the sun in the castle. His body is poised in fine garments and capes, although cold. A small stench radiates from him. His crown remains on his resting head.

I kneel beside him with my mother and my brother. We wear bright white gowns to show the velocity of our sadness.

Later, the funeral procession fills the streets. The bodies of men and women press against each other to get a view of my father's casket. From the carriage, we watch women bellow sobs, and men raise their hands in salute.

"None of them even knew him," my mother sobs.

The cemetery is lush rolling hills. The green grass is vibrant beneath the blue sky. My father should be buried on a day like this.

The priest says some words over my father's body, which resides beneath the wood of a coffin that is draped in purple cloth.

They lower my father into the ground and begin to heap dirt over the coffin.

My brother stays silent. He wears a sash over his suit, sadness and a new future in his eyes.

A WEEK LATER, WE SELL THE ACRES AT auction. One of the town's new young businessmen buys it all.

"How does the Meat Quarry look these days?" he asks me over the table of our legal documents, a flirt in his eyes.

I picture the quarry: faded red, lifeless, dried-up meat.

"You'll see for yourself," I say.

I GUT THE WHITE HOUSE WITH MY brother. My mother goes into town to drink or rests in her bed.

We tear down the curtains, take off the white linens, roll up the rugs. The process takes days. I move through them muted, dismantling every bed, shuffling through photographs, selling off the furniture, piece by piece.

Sometimes in my sweat, I look up at him.

"Don't do anything stupid, OK?" I say.

I stare him deep in the eyes, too, so he knows what I mean.

"You don't do anything stupid either," he says.

He crosses the room, gets close to me, stares into my eyes.

"Promise me," he says. "Say it. Tell me you'll call me if you get any stupid ideas in your head."

A true love swells up in my throat, our bond glimmering and silver between us. I want to sob.

"I promise," I say. "Now you promise, you promise too."

"I promise," he says.

Then we go back to it, back to the slow removal of our family from a place.

THE AIR OF MY FATHER'S OFFICE IS ABAN- doned and stale. No one has been here in some weeks. Dust clings to my fingers when I run my hand over his desk. I sit down in his chair, feel the worn areas his body sunk into.

His drawers are filled with small bits of his life and ours.

I find in succession:

> An old tube of Vaseline
>
> A small velvet pouch with a golden compass inside
>
> A small photograph of a topless woman I do not recognize
>
> A scrap of paper with his handwriting that says: "Remember, they're all assholes and that's got nothing to do with you."

I laugh at the last bit until suddenly I am sobbing.

IN THE LATE AFTERNOONS, I SLIDE INTO my mother's room. My mother sleeps heavily, the sleep of grief. She curls around her knot, only waking to weep and then sleep again.

IN THE LATE AFTERNOONS, I SNEAK THE white pills from my mother's bottle. I am saving again.

GRIEF DESCENDS AND THEN STAYS, A thick black fog around me. The sadness radiates off of me, whispers *death, death, death.*

MY MOTHER'S DRAWERS WERE FILLED with lockets of our baby hair, our small old teeth, small scraps of paper with her lilted handwriting. I could only make out fragments.

in my dripping (pain)
the color of dead grass
someone will remember us
someone in some future time
will think of us
I have lived with a curse

VISION

Six years old in my mother's bed. I wear my favorite pink pajamas. The television rattles off stories before us. Occasionally, my mother curls around me in a brief hug. I can feel our knots touch when she does.

Then she pulls a bag of orange Circus Peanuts from the drawer of her nightstand. This is rare: A sugar, a candy, a treat. The bag seems to glow in the light of the white house.

"Now, now," she says. "We're only going to do this once."

She feeds us both the small sugar sponges, alternating fairly. In my mouth, the sugar dissolves with a joy, melts into my bloodstream and courses through my body. Again, and again, she slides the candy into my mouth, until the bag is empty, until my body is a liquid pile against the bed.

"There, there, isn't that nice? A sweet treat for us today."

Then my stomach clenches up. My body breaks out into a sweat. The sugar has been too much. My mother lets out a small moan.

Together, we crouch on the tile floor of the bathroom, our stomachs twin volcanoes, our knots briefly touching when we writhe.

We take turns erupting together, my mother and I wrenching it up out of ourselves and into the porcelain bowl. For a moment, too short, her hand rests on my back, on the small of my knot.

MY MOTHER MOVES INTO A SMALLER house with my brother, closer to town. I don't mention it, but it nags at me. I hate the idea of them together in this way, aligned.

We unpack the boxes, more long and exhausting days beside each other with the objects of their lives.

For a brief moment, when we're finished, the small house feels fresh and new.

"It's not bad," my brother says. "I can take care of her."

I picture his life stretching on that way, tethered to her wailing, caring for her as she ages.

"You're the better one of us," I say.

WE SPLIT MY FATHER INTO TWO. IT IS A devastating magic trick: Half of the ashes in the first urn, half the ashes in a second urn. I take my half with me. I take what's mine.

He sits in my bag next to me on the train as I reverse my path: The bodies of the deer in the ditches, then the skyscrapers flashing by, no man snoring next to me, until I am back in town.

It is night by the time I unlock my front door. My house has a stale air about it. I have been gone for weeks, mail piled up on the floor near the mouth of the slot.

I ignore all of that. I walk to the bookshelf and place my father there, a few shelves above my head where he can watch me closely.

EACH NIGHT BEFORE BED, I LIFT HIS URN each night and press it against my chest.

This task feels holy, I move slowly, head down in reverence. Then I place his urn back on the shelf. I don't cry anymore.

Grief can be silent.

"Goodnight," I say. "I love you."

Then I kiss the silver.

HENRY CALLS AND LEAVES VOICEMAILS. There are also letters in the mail, the crooked script of his hand reaching out. I ignore it all.

I do see him once in the grocery store. From behind the cover of a shelf, I stare at the back of his neck. I watch how he moves. He seems regular now, the shine gone, everything dulled. My heart is an animal that has vanished, my chest an empty field.

VISION

We are at dinner when Henry dies. I remember the meal very clearly: Steak, red wine, round potatoes. I had forgotten the salad.

"I've forgotten the salad," I say.

This is no surprise. I am often forgetful.

"That's all right now," Henry says.

Henry is as handsome as the day I met him; that thick beard silvered, sparkling eyes, hands which are beautiful to watch as they: Shuffle the bills, touch my body, cut the red meat of the steak with the strong knife.

He forks the cube of steak meat into his mouth. I am still enamored with even his chewing. But suddenly, the jaw stops moving.

"Henry?" I say. "Henry?"

He doesn't respond. Instead, his hands grasp for his heart. I watch his eyes get big, bigger, biggest then he cleaves to the floor.

"Henry!" I scream.

I try the moves from the television shows: I place my mouth on his and breathe in, breathe out. I press two hands hard against his chest. His body trembles beneath mine until it doesn't.

ONCE EVERY FEW MONTHS, MY BROTHER comes to visit me at the cabin.

Here is the routine: I slide my hand into the body of a chicken to remove the organs. I bring them out like wet pearls, purple, red, almost black. They quiver on the table, my favorite small dance.

In the hollow, I put the spices, the replacement. When my brother eats, I am whole again. His eyes glow if the food is good and they are glowing now. Then, his gaze lands on the organs, dry now, matte.

"Why the fuck would you keep those?" he asks, head down, mouth sewn shut, not taking another bite.

On the table, the organs continue to shrink. I love him so much I sob in the bathroom while he does the dishes, the sound of running water covering my warbling, my beautiful brother, my brother, alive, doing the dishes, my brother.

VISION

My brother's face hovering above a birthday cake, exhaling onto the lit candles to extinguish the glow. My hand wrapped around the back of his soft head, pressing his face into the frosting, the sugar all over us both, the laughter pealing up out of our bodies, my god the way I love him, the way I cannot bring myself to say it then.

SOME DAYS, MY MIND TRICKS ME INTO thinking I am still knotted. I run my hand over my abdomen, and a bittersweet river courses through me when I find it flat. I picture the knot constantly, obsessively, as if it is a lost lover. I imagine it with a new life, on a new body, moving through the world without me.

IN THE GROCERY STORE, I FILL A SMALL cart with meat, eggs, spinach. When I touch the meat, the memories come: My father, bloodied up to the elbows. My brother, blood smeared across his cheeks and lips.

"It was a good day in the quarry," my father said, every day at dusk, over and over again, sun setting behind the red mountains of meat, the thick smell of viscera and coin on my tongue, in my throat.

Later, the meat cooks in the pan. I stare down into the blood of it, knowing another man cleaved it up out of the land. I move my mouth against the meat. I cannot taste him there anymore, my father.

NOBODY TOUCHES MY BODY EXCEPT THE strong wind now, which tilts me in various directions depending on the day: north, south, east, west. I stop sleeping. When I glance at the trees outside, I cannot help but count the knots, those unblinking eyes in the brown bark.

THESE ARE DAYS OF NOTHING: SLOW motion, under water, distant from other bodies, other thoughts, other humans. I stop wanting and become very still. I want to cut my life off at the legs.

MY MOTHER COMES TO VISIT FOR TWO nights.

Before she arrives, I clean the house: I scrub the floors, the counters, I clean the bathroom tile and porcelain. I run lemons over the walls.

"Look at you," my mother says, smoking.

When I hug her in greeting, her knot presses against me briefly. A strange disgust rises up in me, a desire to push her away. In horror, I shake the feeling from me.

"Look at you!" I respond.

That night, we eat a simple dinner: Meat, vegetables, red wine. Her face has aged beyond measure, her hair gray, her wrinkles deep.

I reach over and touch her hand. She squeezes mine and we both let out small awkward laughs. It is easier, at times, to touch her than to know her.

THAT NIGHT, WE SHARE MY BED, MY mother and me. It takes on the air of a slumber party, both of us in our pajamas.

Before I turn the lights off, she rolls over to me. She pulls me into a long hug. Her knot presses against me and I warp around the shape of her.

"I do love you," she says.

"Love you too, Mom," I say.

I mean it from a place deep within my ribs. If she notices the wetness from my eyes on her nightgown, she does not mention it.

AFTER MY MOTHER LEAVES, I CANNOT stop crying. For days, my eyes well up without warning, a knowledge between my ribs: I have seen her for the last time.

- Three days after death, the enzymes that were present in the last consumed meal begin to eat the body
- Hearing is the last sense to go when we die
- Certain species of jellyfish are immortal
- Every 40 seconds, a human commits suicide

SOME DAYS I WANT A PAIN GREATER THAN my own grief: the teeth pulled from my mouth, one by one, twenty small labors, my rotted children on a silver tray, my tiny cavities.

Some days, I can hear a parade in the distance: there is joy out in the world, a celebration, confetti, cakes, laughter, not for me.

Some days, I stand on the side of the road, sobbing beneath the sunset: this is waiting for death.

I REMEMBER A TIME BEFORE MY HEART was cratered as the surface of the moon.

IN THE MORNINGS, I FOCUS ON THE URN.

"Good morning, Father," I say.

Outside, the purple sky begins to drop a slow snow upon us. My hands move calmly to make a nice coffee, a small breakfast of an egg and a slice of toast.

The urn gleams at me all the while, a knowing silver eye.

I TEND TO MY SADNESS LIKE A WOUND each day.

I STARE OUT INTO THE STRETCH OF MY backyard, which blends into the foot of my mountain. I can feel the urn watching me as I consider the land, a plan. The eye is hot, metal, probing at my body, trying to enter my thoughts which are of a single silver shovel.

PAIN HAS MADE A PEARL OF ME. I CAN feel the breath of death pulsing, shaping me, making a knot of me again.

VISION

All around me, the world was expanding. Waterfalls were becoming oceans. A snake was devouring fur. Talons were clawing still-pulsing organs. A man and a woman were in love. A woman was giving birth. Another woman was inside of a glass box, chest expanding, ready to die. The woman was me.

IN A SMALL AREA OF FLAT GROUND IN MY backyard, I bring the blade of the shovel to the soil and begin. I use my weight to press it deeper into the earth.

I dig the hole two feet deep just to be sure. The pine trees at the foot of the mountain watching over me, a line of green priests.

The earth smears across my forearms, my fingers caked in dirt. The fresh scent makes my vision sharper, and I move faster.

I glisten sweat from the brow, I feel it pooling at the small of my back. A small mound of dirt piles next to me as I haul more earth out of the ground for my father's grave.

- One of the oldest known burials took place 130,000 years ago
- Certain prehistoric societies de-fleshed the bones of the dead before burial
- In England, those who committed suicide were often buried with stakes through their hearts
- The Anglo-Saxons would often bury groups of urns together, believed to be family members

I PLACE MY FATHER INTO THE MOUTH IN the ground. The silver shimmers out of the dirt in the low sun, metal against soil.

I get back to work, piling dirt in high mounds above his grave so it will settle flat. I know how the land likes to behave. I don't know any prayers. Instead, I nod at the land which holds him, my lost father.

I BRING A SMALL OFFERING TO HIS GRAVE four days later: a small bottle of clear liquor, and the single white antler of a deer I found dead on the roadside, its eye open, reflecting sky, a fleck of blood on the pupil. The fleck of blood is a red so deep it is almost black. I imagine my insides that color and crystalline.

I LIVE IN MY BODY IN MY CABIN AND WAIT for the days to pass and pass and pass, nothing changing, just the way the wind blows the ache inside of me around like dust, and breathe and hurt and hurt, my god, a life of pain pressing sharp against me whether I was knotted or loose as weakened rope.

MY MOTHER CALLS. SOPHIA CALLS. IT IS all the same:

"How are you?"

"Are you OK? You never call."

I keep it pleasant. I keep it light.

"It's so beautiful here. I am so glad I have this cabin."

I imagine myself digging graves to stay calm.

I BEGIN TO FIND THE SMALL BODIES OF birds on the road, the bleached fingers of their bones jutting out wrong, carcasses stuck on the final note of their song. I look at the patterns of their sprawled wings and envy their stillness.

THERE IS SPACE FOR ME, SO I GET THE shovel. I walk to the backyard in my best red dress and stand right beside my father, next to the pile of meats and liquors and antlers I have left for him, which are slowly being eroded by the weather.

I DIG AGAIN, THIS TIME SLOWLY, SPREAD-ing my energy out over the day. I dig with precision, a machine, a perfect rectangle glowing in my mind. I dig without my knot, so my dream was not exactly a prophecy.

DOWN, DOWN INTO THE EARTH, THE repetition of my body against the land. The mound of dirt next to me is big, a mass, the friendly scent of earth in the nostrils.

By the time I am finished, the fat bright body of the sun has begun its drop, that purple twilight emerging above my head.

VISION

We are young. We are holding hands on a cold bright spring day. We are swimming in the river. We are making love in the Meat Quarry for the first time. We are eating a burger and splitting the fries. We are walking through the art museum. We are warm in bed. We are eating cakes and then kissing. We are standing beside the lake. We are eating a beautiful dinner. We are reciting facts to each other. We are twined around each other on a Sunday morning. We are reciting vows to each other. We are looking at our daughter. We are growing old, side by side.

AFTER THE WHITE PILLS FILL MY MOUTH,

I climb down into the earth, my hole, the scent of soil all around me, face up to the night above me, navy, dark, stars stationed and shimmering.

I can feel my father beside me, my mother and brother in the distance. I lie in the dirt and wait.

VISION

We are eating dinner around the table in the white house on The Acres. We are selling the meat in town. We are riding in the truck to the river. We are shouting out the years from the tombstones in the cemetery. We are walking in the cold light of the full moon. We are singing happy birthday to my brother. We are harvesting the meat from the quarry. We are eating Circus Peanuts. We are laughing at my father's joke. We are gathered around my daughter's crib where she is dreaming. We have no knot among us. We are laughing from deep in our bellies. We know joy.

THE SKY OPENS UP AND SWIRLS ABOVE me, a blur of stars streaking out from a pure white pinprick in the center.

I blink to clear my vision. When I open my eyes, the light is only stronger and more luminous. The sky throbs and streams with color, rivers of shimmering green and blue and white against the dark night.

The beauty of the brightness makes tears flow down my cheeks. I know now that I was wrong: The maw of the world was never metal. It was always light.

The brilliance illuminates each black cavern inside of me, smoothing the deep craters in my heart. My ears fail and my eyes widen, all pain finally gone, offering myself up to the wide, bright mouth of death.

A NOTE ON FACTS

The facts in this book were compiled and edited from a variety of sources online, with special thanks to: Wikipedia, WebMD, *Smithsonian Magazine*, *The New York Times*, *The New Yorker*, *National Geographic*, The March of Dimes, Healthline, LiveScience, and countless others.

A NOTE ON PREVIOUS PUBLICATIONS

Early pieces of this novel were first published in *Salt Hill Journal*, *Triangle House*, *The Fiddleback*, *Everyday Genius*, *New York Tyrant*, *littletell*, and *darkfuckingwizard*. Thank you to the editors for their support.

ACKNOWLEDGEMENTS

For my family, first and forever. Love you big.

For being my first readers, and being kind at the right time: Jaime Fountaine, Maria Flaccavento, Ginger Rudolph, and Blake Butler. For their artistic support: Alda Sigurðardóttir & Kristveig Halldórsdóttir of the Gullkistan Residency in Iceland, where the first draft was written. For their hard work: Eric & Elizajane Obenauf, and everyone at Two Dollar Radio who made it real.

For their friendship & kindness: Missy Meyers & Demian Fenton, Susan Johnson, Katie Reing, Julie Schuchard, Allisone & David Brussin, JT Cobell, Edward & Sara Francks, Michael Thursby Kerchner, Alicia LaPann, Annie Liontas, Clare & Ted Cotugno, Mike Kitchell & Dean Smith, Caroline Crew, Carlos the Rollerblader, Michael Kimball, Sara McCorriston, Roxane Gay, Melissa Broder, Amelia Gray, Simon Jacobs, Scott McClanahan, Samantha Irby, Kent D. Wolf, Julia Bloch, Colin Winnette, Peter LaBerge, Jeff Jackson, Tommy Pico, Carmen Maria Machado, Erica Dawson, Olivier Desmettre, Véronique Béghain.

For the friends who loved and supported me while I fought through this book when it felt impossible: *Thank you.*

SARAH ROSE ETTER is the author of *Tongue Party*, and *The Book of X*, her first novel, which is the winner of the 2019 Shirley Jackson Award for novel. Her work has appeared or is forthcoming in *Guernica*, *BOMB*, *Gulf Coast*, *The Cut*, *VICE*, and more. She has been awarded residences at the Jack Kerouac House, the Disquiet International program in Portugal, and the Gullkistan Writing Residency in Iceland. In 2017, she was the keynote speaker at the Society for the Study of American Women Writers conference in Bordeaux, France, where she presented on surrealist writing as a mode of feminism. She earned her B.A. in English from Pennsylvania State University and her M.F.A. in Fiction from Rosemont College. She lives in Austin, TX.

BOOK CLUB & READER GUIDE

Written by Sarah Rose Etter

We hope the following list of discussion questions will enhance your exploration of Sarah Rose Etter's debut novel, *The Book of X*. They are meant to stimulate your discussion, offer new points of view, and enrich your experience with the novel.

This and other Two Dollar Radio reader guides—as well as additional material like interviews, book trailers, excerpts, and full lists of reviews—can be found on our website, twodollarradio.com.

Enjoy!

BOOK CLUB & READER GUIDE

Questions and Topics for Discussion:

1. Much of *The Book of X* is focused on Cassie, the main character, being born in the shape of a knot, a hereditary condition passed down from the female side of her family. What parallels can you draw between this surreal physical condition and your body? Do you find the idea of the knot to be effective as a literary device? Why or why not?

2. Cassie's relationship with her mother is marked with difficulty, as her mother constantly attempts to "improve" her—whether through weight loss, dresses, or new makeup. How would you have improved or distanced yourself from this relationship if you were Cassie? Are the actions of the mother enough to warrant the ending of that relationship? Do Cassie and her mother love each other?

3. The Meat Quarry represents a forbidden place to Cassie for much of the book. When she's finally allowed into the Meat Quarry, it turns out she's excellent at harvesting. What did you think the Meat Quarry represented? How did the Meat Quarry function as both a place and a character in the novel?

4. Cassie's relationship with her father is much warmer than that with her mother. They laugh and joke, despite his drinking. Does Cassie have a real relationship with her father, or are they more like friends? What role does his death play—and why does it impact her so greatly?

5. Throughout the book, Cassie is haunted by visions of another life—one which she describes as better than her current life. However, those visions often veer into the horrifying. How did her visions drive the story for you? What impact did they have

on your understanding of her as a character? Which visions were the most impactful?

6. After Cassie moves to the city, she is forced to adjust her understanding of the world. How does this change in location impact her mentality? What does the city represent to Cassie? Have you ever moved to a new place and felt the same displacement Cassie faces?

7. Cassie's relationship with men throughout the book is marked with assault, rejection, and finally love. How do these different experiences shape her as a person? Does her relationship with Henry represent real love, imaginary love, or flawed love? How does love function throughout the book as a part of Cassie's life? Do you relate to her experiences? Are there right or wrong ways to love someone?

8. After her surgery, Cassie believes her life will improve. How does Cassie's relationship to her body change or stay the same after surgery? Is there any marked difference in her life? How is her surgery a rejection of her lineage? How are our bodies a reflection of ourselves—and how are they not?

9. Surrealism plays a major part in the portrayal of Cassie's life. How did you respond to this technique? What imagery or scenes resonated with you? How did surrealism help or hurt the plot of the novel?

10. The death of Cassie's father leads to the final outcome of the book. Why was his death such a pivotal moment for her? How could she have faced her own pain differently?